HOMELESS for the Holidays

What Others Are Saying About Homeless for the Holidays

A classic tale for modern times, *Homeless for the Holidays* offers gladdening and humorous assurance that the best things in life have nothing to do with things. Add this heartwarming story to your favorite holiday traditions.

—**Richard Paul Evans**, #1 *New York Times* Bestselling Author of forty-three books including *The Christmas Box.*

Most of the world is one paycheck from poverty. If you have been to the brink, skated near to losing it all, or wondered how someone ended up in such a hard place, you will cheer, cry, and feel with each member of the Baker family. *Homeless for the Holidays* helps you think through, pray through, and navigate your own life's priorities. If you want the holidays and life's everydays to reflect what is most meaningful, this is the book for you—and all those you love.

—**Pam Farrel**, author of forty-five books including bestselling *Men Are Like Waffles, Women are Like Spaghetti, Ten Best Decisions A Parent Can Make*, and *Ten Best Decisions A Couple Can Make.*

Homeless for the Holidays updates the timeless script from the classic film, *It's A Wonderful Life* in a way that is bluntly honest, deeply moving, and scary. This is the story of a family sacrificing everything they hold dear only to discover something that is really worth holding onto. Because what happened to the Bakers happens to hundreds each week across the country, this novel is not just inspiring and uplifting, it is an important testament to the fragile times in which we live and why the love of family is more vital now than ever.

—**Ace Collins**, award-winning author of ninety books including the *In the President's Service* series.

A true-to-life story that left me full of emotion, long after I turned the last page. The Bakers could easily be you or me. When tragedy strikes, the family experiences a long road of heartache that transforms their hearts to reflect the true spirit of Christmas. A touching holiday story of redemption that will please readers, both young and old.

—**Ginny Hartman**, international bestselling author of historical romance including the *Ladies of Deception* series and *The Unconventional Suitors* series.

I admit—I am a Christmas-aholic! *Homeless for the Holidays* warms the heart, and reminds us where joy comes from and how to share that joy with others. Buy copies for the people in your life who are struggling with finding the joy of the season.

—**Carol McLeod**, best-selling author of nine books including *Pass the Joy, Please* and *Guide Your Mind, Guard Your Heart, Grace Your Tongue*.

Homeless for the Holidays is a poignant but delightful story of a family who, through no fault of their own, loses everything they once thought mattered—only to find those things that truly do. I thoroughly enjoyed this book and recommend it wholeheartedly to anyone who enjoys characters with heart and stories with a purpose.

—**Kathi Macias**, award-winning author of more than fifty books, including *Unexpected Christmas Hero*.

Traumatic losses like job termination, mounting debt, family tension, hopelessness, and depression can be closer to home than we think. PeggySue Wells does a masterful job telling this story of burgeoning trials that compel a family to seek the silver lining in every circumstance. Readers will value the life lesson that we learn what matters most when we have endured some of the most painful scenarios imaginable.

—**Michele Howe**, author of twenty-one books including *Navigating the Friendship Maze*.

I loved *Homeless for the Holidays*. This is an enjoyable and excellent read with unpredictable twists and turns. This story is a great reminder that life can change in an instant and that family is more important than material possessions.

—**Crystal Bowman**, best-selling, award-winning author of one hundred books including *Our Daily Bread for Kids* and *M is for Manger.*

I absolutely loved this book. *Homeless for the Holidays* is a wonderful heartfelt Christmas story with a message of hope for families in, and through, the tough times. The Baker family learns what it means to place 'Christ' back in their Christmas and the importance of gratitude for the important things in life.

—**Jayme Lee Hull**, host of *Face To Face Mentoring* Podcast, author of *Face To Face: Discover How Mentoring Can Change Your Life.*

PeggySue masterfully weaves a story of terrible loss that reveals what is most important in life. I was inspired by her tale of love, redemption, and discovery.

—**Susan G. Mathis**, author of *The Fabric of Hope: An Irish Family Legacy.*

Homeless for the Holidays is a poignant story of a family's struggle to embrace the things that truly matter in life. Readers will see themselves in the challenges the Bakers face and become cheerleaders for this family to overcome their problems. Well-written and engaging, this is an inspiring story for any time of the year, and once you begin this journey with the Bakers, you won't stop until it's over.

—**Linda Gilden**, author of *Words to Live By: 52 Ordinary Words that Lead to an Extraordinary Life.*

HOMELESS for the Holidays

By

P.S. Wells
and
Marsha Wright

One family learns what is truly important when they lose it all and find they have everything.

Adapted from the screenplay by

George Johnson

Cover and Interior Design: Derinda Babcock
Editor(s): Sue Fairchild, Deb Haggerty

PUBLISHED BY: Elk Lake Publishing, Inc., 35 Dogwood Dr., Plymouth, MA 02360, 2018

Library Cataloging Data

Names: Wells, P. S. and Wright, Marsha (P. S. Wells and Marsha Wright)

Homeless for the Holidays / P. S. Wells and Marsha Wright
184 p. 23cm × 15cm (9in × 6 in.)

Description: Christmas is coming, and Jack Baker's finances, friends, and future are as gone as last year's holiday. One year ago, Jack Baker had it all—a beautiful family, a lucrative career, and a generous bonus to spend on the annual Baker family Christmas extravaganza. Now the Bakers are homeless, and clueless about what to do next. Amidst the holiday traditions and trappings, one family learns what is truly important when they lose all they have and find they have everything.

Identifiers: ISBN-13: 978-1-948888-48-6 (trade) | 49-3 (POD)
| 978-1-948888-50-9 (e-book.)

Key Words: 1. Homeless, 2. Family, 3. Bankruptcy, 4. Relationships, 5. Contemporary, 6. Redemption, 7. Loss of Job

LCCN: 2018953654 Fiction

Dedication

To our readers.
May you find what is truly important
because the best cannot be taken away.

Chapter One

NOVEMBER 12, 2010

"Here they come!" Jack Baker elbowed his slouching son. "You know the drill. Assume your positions."

"Yeah, yeah." Twelve-year-old Adam twirled his elf hat on his index finger. "Where would the community be without the Baker family's annual Christmas display?"

Jack's wife, Sheryl, looped her arm through her husband's. "People tell me all the time that we are part of their Christmas tradition. Their holiday is not complete until they see the Baker residence."

In the dinnertime darkness, a light sedan turned down the quiet subdivision street and slowly drove toward the Baker's house.

"Everyone smile!" Sheryl licked her thumb and rubbed the remains of hot chocolate from the corner of her daughter's mouth.

"Gross, Mom!" Nearly ten, Michelle pulled away and wiped her long sleeve across her face. "I'm not a little kid anymore."

"I know, dear." Sheryl knelt in front of Kim and brushed dark bangs from the preschooler's forehead.

Through his teeth, Jack blew a warning whistle.

"Did you spring a leak, Dad?" Adam returned his dad's elbow to the ribs.

Jack nodded toward the car. "They're nearly here. Get ready everyone. And smile."

Sheryl quickly surveyed her family. "Be sure to wave big for the photo."

Dressed in elaborate Santa and Mrs. Claus costumes, Jack and Sheryl Baker proudly posed with their three children between the stately pillars on the front porch steps as the car drew near to their address. Fresh fallen snow blanketed the ground on this cold November night in Wooded Falls, Michigan, proof that nature had harmonized with Jack's decorating efforts to create the postcard perfect effect. As perfect as could be with squirming offspring.

Dressed as an elf, Adam's eyes crossed as he watched his breath turn to small clouds. Also in an elf costume, Michelle shivered. Bundled in a snowsuit under her costume, three-year-old Kim balanced on tiptoes in front of her beaming parents. Peeking out of a brightly decorated Christmas box, she tugged at the bow clipped to her straight hair and peered expectantly at the approaching visitor.

Known as the Crown of the Cul-de-sac, the Baker house was a brilliant display of Christmas splendor. For the past decade, the Bakers had received the town's "Best Christmas Décor" award, and this year would be no exception. Jack spent every dime of his annual $5,000 bonus on the holiday, and each year, the photographer cruised by to take their picture for the feature section of the newspaper.

"Daddy, I'm cold!" Heavy snowflakes collected on Michelle's hunched shoulders.

Jack spoke through his frozen smile. "Just a few more seconds, sweetie. Is everybody waving?"

On cue, the Baker family waved energetically as the car braked in front of their house. The driver's automatic window slowly inched down just far enough for the oversized lens of the camera to brave the cold and focus on them.

"I'll bet you a pair of mukluks he has his heater on full blast." Adam spoke through chattering teeth.

Then the camera disappeared inside the warmth of the photojournalist's window, followed by a friendly toot of the horn, and the vehicle swung around the cul-de-sac. Stopping briefly for a second look, the car left the way it had come, red tail lights blending with the lights that illuminated the Baker's walkway.

"And that's just the beginning," Adam predicted.

"Opening night." Jack glanced at his wristwatch. "After the dinner hour, this street will be bumper to bumper with sightseers who consider our Baker extravaganza the eighth wonder of the Christmas season."

"A drive by." Adam saluted as the photographer's car turned the corner and disappeared.

Jack rubbed his gloved hands together. "Okay, that's enough. Everyone inside." He scooped up Kim in her oversized box, and trailed Sheryl as she retreated into the warmth of the house with the children close behind.

Adam brought up the rear. "Where would the Baker family be without our yearly holiday display?"

Chapter Two

Sheryl breathed in the seasonal scent of fresh pine and spices as the family paraded inside the Baker's tri-level house. Décor magazines and home tours for community fundraisers frequently featured their residence and the jewel-tone interior. She and Jack were immensely proud of the living environment they had created.

Jack's office flanked the entryway on the right with the formal dining room to the left. Straight ahead, large windows in the vaulted living room framed a view of the placid pond at the edge of their manicured backyard.

Followed by her impatient brother, Michelle led the way down the stairs to the family room and the ceiling-high Christmas tree ablaze with no less than two thousand miniature white lights.

Earlier, Sheryl had spread the dining table with fresh citrus, bottles of spices, pungent cinnamon sticks, and yards of ribbon. While Bing Crosby sang "I'm Dreaming of a White Christmas" from the sound system, the three children pushed cloves into oranges and tied ribbon bows around bundled cinnamon sticks. Now, the fragrant homemade ornaments hung on the tree. The ones Kim had helped with dangled in a clumped bunch on the bottom front branch. The sagging bough, heavy with her collection, delighted the young toddler.

Pushing past his sister, Adam tossed his pointed elf hat under the Christmas tree and ran to the fireplace. He sat cross-legged and held his hands toward the crackling heat. Above him, five stockings hung at a whimsical angle, waiting for Christmas Eve when they would be overstuffed with thoughtful gifts for each family member.

Jack toted Kim to the coffee table where he steadied the cumbersome box-shaped costume as Sheryl pulled. With a flourish, Kim popped out of the restricting costume. Her legs were moving before Jack set her down and Sheryl snatched the bow from her black hair as the small girl sped to the fireplace and dropped into Adam's lap.

Jack and Sheryl removed their red velvet coats. "Honey, turn on the radio," Sheryl called to Michelle.

Michelle eyed Sheryl's abandoned guitar case leaning against the wall. "Mom, can we sing some Christmas carols?"

With a guilty twinge, Sheryl glanced at the case and shook her head. "Maybe tomorrow. Okay?"

Michelle's expression reflected her disappointment, and Sheryl made a mental note to add singing Christmas carols to their already packed holiday schedule. Tonight she and Jack were going to finish addressing the stack of Christmas cards.

Obediently, Michelle dialed in a music station. From the coffee table, she then retrieved the Baker Family Christmas photo album and dropped down cross-legged next to her brother.

Sheryl slipped an arm around Jack's waist. "Honey, let's—"

Jack's cell phone interrupted the mood with the sound of "Silver Bells." He fished the phone from his pocket. "The document you're looking for should be in your inbox," said Jack in response to the caller's question. "I emailed that one this morning. Around ten … Nope, that's the one I sent yesterday."

With a roll of her eyes, Sheryl turned her attention away from her husband's one-way business conversation. She bent over Michelle's shoulder as the girl thumbed through the thick pages that framed memories of previous Christmases. When had she found time to put the album together? Life must have been slower in past years.

Michelle pointed to a familiar favorite photo. Covered with blue and white bulbs and silver tinsel, the top of the Baker's first Christmas tree had barely reached Jack's shoulders. That was the last year anything about the Baker's Christmas décor had been small. This year's ten-foot tree stood laden with a multitude of bright ornaments suspended from the plump branches and topped with a blazing star.

"You're looking for the one that says update," Jack instructed over the phone. "Yes! You got it? Great. Take a look at it."

Sheryl knew how most of these phone calls led to another. Would business steal another evening of Jack's time? Couldn't this wait until tomorrow? She glanced at the clock. In another five minutes, she would start filling out the Christmas card list by herself.

Michelle giggled when she turned to the next page of the photo album. A younger Jack and Sheryl held newborn Adam dressed in a miniature reindeer outfit. Baby Adam's eyes were crossed as he tried to focus on his blinking red nose.

Sheryl turned to beckon Jack over to see, but he was already punching numbers into his cell phone. She resigned herself to addressing this year's Christmas cards by herself. Leafing a few pages forward, Michelle found her first Christmas. In a red dress and matching hat, her blonde curls spilled out around the edges as baby Michelle gave a toothless smile. She took the album to show her dad, but Jack gave a plastic smile and pointed at the cell phone pressed to his ear. Sheryl waved Michelle back to her seat by the fireplace. Michelle elbowed her brother to show him the photo, but Adam gave only a cursory glance while pawing through the box of Christmas candies and racing Kim for his favorites.

The next Polaroid, one of her favorites, made Sheryl grin.

"Mom," Michelle's cheeks reddened. "I wish you would take this one out."

"What?" Adam craned his neck to get a glimpse of the album. Michelle tipped the book out of his sight. The portrait showed baby Michelle stretched out on a white fur blanket, wearing a Santa hat, and nothing else.

"Just turn the page." Sheryl wrapped an arm around her daughter's shoulder.

Flipping to the back of the album, Michelle found last year's photos from Kim's first Christmas with them. The Bakers had adopted Kim when she was two years old. Sheryl had dressed the toddler in a green velvet dress with a white collar trimmed in holly leaves. Kim's almond-shaped eyes stared full of wonder at a furry teddy bear larger than her. Already, the little girl had appeared overwhelmed by the Bakers's Christmas celebration.

Chapter Three

November 26, 2010

"Look out!" Sheryl jerked her shopping cart to the side.

A frenzied shopper with an overloaded cart nearly rear-ended Adam as he dropped an armload of sale items into his mother's equally stuffed cart.

Jumping out of the way, Adam gave his mother a knowing look. "And you won't let me drive."

Despite the early morning hour, the aisles at the local big box store resembled a bumper car attraction as shoppers careened their way down the crowded rows, stocking up on the day after Thanksgiving holiday sales.

"People should watch what they're doing." Sheryl ran her cart into the sneakered heels of a woman as she reached overhead for the latest model air popcorn popper. "Sorry." Embarrassed, Sheryl angled her cart away from the wounded shopper, who glared as she rubbed her ankle.

Rounding a corner, Sheryl barely avoided a collision with another cart. Jack's.

"Progress?"

He kissed her cheek. "So far, so good."

In the child seat of Jack's cart, Kim bounced up and down. "Mommy!"

Michelle handed the newspaper ads to Kim to better inspect Sheryl and Adam's finds.

Jack scanned the holiday specials in Kim's hand, matching the circled items with the articles they had collected. "Molly Mittens. Did you get the Molly Mittens?"

"Shhhh." Sheryl quickly looked at Michelle and breathed a sigh of relief. Adam and Michelle had moved down the aisle to the DVD rack. Michelle hadn't heard him. She lowered her voice. "Got 'em. And two Safari Vacation Kits—one for us and one for the Sunday school gift exchange. Did you get the reversible plastic glove liners?"

Jack searched through his stash and triumphantly held the package in the air. “Check. Who are these for?”

Sheryl shook her head. “Can’t remember. We’ll figure it out—they’re eighty percent off. Did you get the V-Slam Gaming System?”

He heaved a defeated sigh. “Struck out. They were already gone.”

Sheryl shifted her cart to the side of the aisle. “The kids will be disappointed. The V-Slam is the popular thing now, and they planned to play during the holiday break from school.”

A shopper squeezed past, a V-Slam System perched on the top of her merchandise.

“Whoa.” Jack stepped in front of the cart. “Where did you find the gaming system?”

The woman smiled in triumph. “In the sporting goods section.” She pointed behind her. “There was still one left a minute ago.”

Immediately several shoppers, including Jack and Sheryl, swung their carts toward the sporting goods department. Jockeying for position, they began to race.

Chapter Four

Just before noon, the exuberant Baker family exited the discount store. Jack felt blissful as he led the procession. His fully loaded shopping cart contained Kim in the child's seat. Michelle and Adam followed while Sheryl brought up the rear with her own over-stuffed cart in the annual Baker parade.

Spotting the Salvation Army Santa ringing his bell in their path, Jack's smile sagged. Glancing about, he sought an alternate route but found no options. "We have to pass him," he grumbled.

"Just go." Sheryl pushed her cart beside her husband.

Passing the Santa, Kim laughed and pointed to the brightly clanging bell.

"Merry Christmas, little one." Santa gave a slight bow.

"Dad?" Michelle tugged expectantly on his arm.

Jack reached into his pocket and pulled out his loose change. He sorted through the coins, returned the quarters to his pocket, and dropped a few pennies and nickels into Michelle's hand. Jack did a quick mental calculation, satisfied to be throwing away only thirty-seven cents.

Sheepishly, Michelle dropped the coins into the red bucket.

"Thank you, young lady." Santa smiled.

"Come on, Michelle." Jack wanted to put this awkward feeling behind him.

"Bless you for your generosity. If we all give just a little, a great deal of good can be accomplished." Santa nodded to Jack. "Good sir, may your heart be forever changed from this day forward."

"Yeah, right." Jack herded his family and the pair of unwieldy carts to the parking lot and away from Santa.

Walking next to Sheryl, he frowned back at the red clad bell ringer. "Why do they let people stand outside and make customers feel guilty about purchasing gifts for their families? The idea lacks business sense."

"Hon, let it go." Sheryl nodded toward the three pairs of eyes watching their exchange. "Please, Jack." She smiled and raised her voice. "Where do we go next? We don't want to lose one moment of this day."

Jack wasn't to be deterred. He stopped walking to emphasize his point. "Homeless people don't need my money. What they need is to get a job." He pounded on the shopping cart handle, and Kim quickly pulled away her fingers. "I work hard for my money. If they don't work, they shouldn't expect to have any."

"Okay, sweetie. Now you're sounding cold and mean. You've done much to help people." She lifted Kim from the shopping cart and hugged the child to her. She looked meaningfully at Jack as she settled the hood of Kim's coat over her small head. "Remember?"

After months of paperwork and tortuous waiting, Jack and Sheryl had brought Kim home from an orphanage in China. The unanimous and welcome addition to their perfect family, Kim doubled as the couple's way to make a difference in at least one life. A difference in the world.

Jack patted the top of the hooded head of his youngest. "Exactly. Let people decide how they want to give, don't guilt them into it."

"Can we please just finish shopping?" Sheryl pushed her cart forward again with Kim forked on her hip.

Jack shrugged. He was being a jerk and he knew it. He looked around and saw Sheryl going the wrong way. "This way." He hooked a thumb in the other direction.

One-handed, his wife turned her cart and groaned when the wheels caught against a patch of rough ice.

"Adam," she called.

Adam quickly gripped the troublesome cart and pulled. Sheryl pushed. Ice chipped, the wheels sprang free, and the hard-won V-Slam System toppled into the dirty parking lot slush with a wet thud.

"Uh-oh," Kim exclaimed.

"Jack," Sheryl called.

Jack groaned and handed off his cart to Michelle. He picked up the boxed game and brushed off the dirty snow. He balanced the soggy V-Slam back in his wife's cart and wiped his hands on his pants. Lifting Kim from Sheryl's arms, he put the little girl back in the front of his cart. Kim protested and reached for her mother. In a practiced move, Jack distracted the toddler by handing her his keys to play with. Leading the way, he carved a path through the slush and snow accumulating in the busy parking lot.

Suddenly, down the row of parked cars, lights flashed and a horn blared.

"Somebody needs to control—" Jack located the parked van making the racket. Then he narrowed his eyes. "Hey, that's ours!"

"Shopping and a show," Adam commented as Jack grabbed his keys from Kim and pressed the button that stopped the offending noise.

When he reached the van, Jack swung open the rear door. With an air of the returning conqueror, he triumphantly transferred the packages, pausing to admire the V-Slam Gaming System. He had outmaneuvered several other shoppers to get to this baby. His victorious smile dimmed as he wiped the residue of dirty slush from one side. Shrugging, he added this item to the others carefully packed into the back of the van.

Sheryl reached the car, and he unloaded her cart. He seamlessly picked up his earlier conversation. "People who don't make an effort to work shouldn't spoil the holidays for us hardworking types. They should—"

"Honey, please." Sheryl touched his arm. "Don't spoil this day for us."

He closed his eyes and nodded. "You're right. I'm sorry." He leaned over and kissed her on the forehead just as his cell phone rang. Glancing at the caller ID, he mouthed, "I love you," and put the phone to his ear. "This is Jack."

"I love you, too," she said.

Jack straightened. "Mr. Fergusson, hi." Jack listened and then moaned. "Oh, you know what? It's on my desk. Can I get the paperwork to you first thing Monday morning?" He paused, hopeful. "Right now?"

Beside him, Sheryl inhaled sharply. Sensing a brewing crisis, Adam and Michelle gathered around.

"Yeah, no problem," responded Jack breezily. As Sheryl and the kids pressed closer, he stepped back. Holding the phone high against his ear, he backed himself against the van.

Sheryl stood staring at him—Kim on one hip, and her hand planted firmly on the other. His eyes pleaded his apology while his lips curled into a fake smile to accompany the words he spoke into the phone. "Sure. I'll be there in fifteen minutes."

He clicked off his phone. Looking at the four pairs of eyes that met his, he shrugged. "I forgot to sign the Allison contract. I've got to run in and take care of it. It'll just take a minute."

"A real minute or a 'just a minute?'" Adam wanted to know.

Sheryl shook her head knowingly. "It never takes just a minute. The moment you walk through that door, it's going to be like any other day to your boss and he's going to have more work for you to do."

Michelle tugged at his arm. "Does this mean we can't shop anymore?"

Adam turned away and kicked at a clod of dirty ice.

"You have to understand ..." Jack's gut churned with the familiar and sickening pull between family and work. He also knew which side of the conflict would cut him slack and which side would not.

"I know." Sheryl's voice was flat. "You have to go."

Jack pulled both empty carts toward a collection site. "He needs that contract, and the mistake was mine."

"Load up, kids." Sheryl secured Kim in her car seat and closed the door. She turned to Jack. "You know what I want for Christmas?"

"Tell me." Jack felt relieved she wasn't giving him the silent treatment.

"You."

He frowned, confused.

She leaned into his chest. "I wish the phone would stop ringing and that you'd spend some uninterrupted time with your beautiful wife and charming children. Even if only for a few days."

He wrapped his arms around her. "Yeah, me, too. Problem is, if my phone wasn't ringing, we'd be bumming Santa for peanut butter. Look, it's going to happen. Soon. And then I'll have all kinds of ridiculous time for lounging around the pool with you and the kids."

She sighed. "I just sometimes wonder how many years we'll lose before it happens."

"We've talked about this. I have to position myself for that lifestyle by putting in the extra effort now." He lifted her chin to look into her eyes. "Really. I have no choice."

Chapter Five

"Kimmy, you're too big for Mommy to carry." Sheryl panted as she set Kim in the vestibule of the church. Wide and warm, the entryway looked to be in bloom with potted scarlet poinsettias. Dressed in their Sunday best, congregation members greeted one another as they hurried inside, deposited winter wraps on the coat racks that occupied one wall, and dispersed to age-appropriate Sunday school classrooms.

Michelle and Adam followed their mom through the doorway and stomped snow from their shoes. Adam quickly threw his jacket on the top of the coat rack and hurried away to join a group of boys.

Sheryl smiled as she watched Michelle remove her gloves and tuck them into her coat pockets. Her children were all different. How much is gender and how much is inherent temperament? She stooped to unbutton the oversized buttons on Kim's coat.

"If she's too heavy, why did you carry her, Mommy?" Michelle unwrapped her holiday neck scarf. "Kim can walk."

"I didn't want her shoes to get messy in the snow and salt." Sheryl slipped Kim's coat from her shoulders. "After Sunday school, be sure you come here right away. We don't want to be late for worship. The back seats quickly fill up."

Sheryl looked up as a gust of wind and Jack blew through the door. "Wow, that didn't take long."

"Found a spot near the front. A bit of luck, I'd say." Jack held the door for an elderly couple who followed him inside.

Sheryl kissed Jack's cheek. "I'll take Kim to her class and be right back."

"I can take her." Michelle reached for Kim's hand.

Eager to talk with several friends who were clustered together, Sheryl agreed. "Great. Thanks, honey."

Michelle turned to her father. "Dad, I need money for the Children's Community Need Fund."

Jack rolled his eyes as he shed his overcoat. "Everyone needs money these days."

"Hey, Dad." Adam dashed up with two friends in tow. "I need money for the Children's Community Fund."

"You too?"

Adam lowered his voice so his friends couldn't hear. "Everybody else is giving."

Jack looked from Michelle to Adam, and glanced down at Kim who extended her hand, her large, dark eyes saying more than words could express. He sighed and dug into his pocket. "All right, we wouldn't want you kids to look bad in front of your friends." He dropped three dimes, a nickel, and two pennies into Adam's hand.

Adam swiftly pocketed the small amount of coins before his friends could see and shouldered past them on his way to Sunday school.

Into Michelle's hand, Jack deposited two pennies, three nickels and a dime and then pressed two nickels into Kim's outstretched palm.

"Uh, thanks, Dad." Michelle gave an embarrassed glance at her mom. Spotting her friend, Michelle brightened as Barbara Ann joined them. With a cheery smile, Barbara Ann took Kim's other hand and the two girls led Kim through the lobby to class. Sheryl shrugged and made her way to the women gathered in animated conversation by the coffee urns at the welcome desk.

Chapter Six

December 25, 2010

Murmuring voices woke Jack. Lying still, he listened. Adam and Michelle were in the hall. Then the sound of running feet in footed pajamas padded down the stairs and rounded the corner. He heard Kim join her siblings, squealing with delight.

Hearing his children whisper outside the bedroom door, Jack stretched and fluffed the pillow beneath his head. Light filtered around the edges of the window blinds. The digital clock read 8:10 a.m. Most Christmas mornings they were up by now, but this Christmas he had slept late.

"Shhhhh," he heard from the hall. Only Adam could wake people by telling his sisters to be quiet. Jack smiled, certain that was Adam's calculated intent.

On the dresser, tiny lights on a miniature Christmas tree illuminated the ceramic nativity scene. Mary knelt beside the crèche where the infant Christ slept while Joseph stood watch over his family, the fulfillment of hundreds of years of prophecy. A lamb across his shoulders, the statue of a shepherd stood adoring from a distance, and the magi in colorful robes and bearing gifts knelt near the manger. Wearing a Mona Lisa smile, a representative of the heavenly choir looked upon the scene.

Beside Jack, Sheryl slept soundly, her breathing shallow and even. She had worked hard to make a perfect Christmas for her family. Last night, Jack and Sheryl had been up until the wee hours piling packages under the tree, filling sequined stockings, and mixing up the breakfast casserole. Jack had put fresh batteries in the video camera. They were set and ready for this morning's grand celebration of Jesus's birth that took place so many years ago in a simple Bethlehem stable. The arrival of the Christ child into humble surroundings continued to impact the globe to the present day.

Jack heard the children again. They were impatient to get to the best part of the day—the unwrapping of the gifts. According to the Baker family rule, the children could come down from their upstairs bedrooms to the main level on Christmas morning, but no one could go to the lower level family room where the gifts were waiting stacked under the tree until they received the go ahead from their parents. Just thinking of the fun, the packages, and the good food to come rapidly chased residual sleepiness from Jack's brain. He felt as eager to get downstairs as the kids.

Jack fidgeted. He tossed. He checked Sheryl again, but she slept on. He sighed and sat up, his impatience no longer controllable. Behind him, he heard Sheryl giggle. He swung around, realizing he had been tricked. She had been awake all this time, listening to the subdued Christmas morning chatter of the children, and humored by her husband's similar impatience. He playfully tossed his pillow at her head. Laughing, she rolled away.

"I wondered how long you'd be able to wait." Getting up, she reached for her robe. "I can hear the children are as impatient as you."

Minutes later, in robes and slippers, he and Sheryl waited in the family room, camera and video camera in hand. The lights on the Christmas tree sparkled, a fire blazed, and Christmas music played through the sound system. From the kitchenette came the full-bodied aroma of French-press coffee.

"Okay." Jack called up the staircase. "You can come down now."

Three screaming children pounded down the steps and swung around the corner. In a flash, they were across the room grabbing presents and reading the nametags. Quickly, the room filled wall to wall with colorful wrapping paper, ribbons, empty boxes, and gifts embraced and set aside. The air reverberated with shrieks of glee and "thank you."

Sheryl handed Jack a full mug and sat on the oversized couch next to him. In salute, he tapped his cup against hers.

"Well done, Mrs. Baker."

"Thank you, Mr. Baker." She sipped her coffee, flavored with peppermint cream. "This is my favorite time of year."

"Mine, too." Jack kissed his wife. "And you and the children are my favorite people in the entire world to celebrate Christmas with."

Jack pulled Kim, and the new doll she cuddled, onto his lap. Kim told him the dolly's name as his cell phone rang. Jack retrieved his phone from his robe pocket.

"Baker here."

Sheryl held out her arms and Kim shifted onto her mother's lap. Removing her new ear buds, Michelle walked over and gazed sadly at her dad. Jack waved her back to her many new gifts, but she remained, looking pointedly at the phone. He gestured that she should listen to her music. When she indicated he should return the phone to his pocket, he shifted his attention back to the caller.

"Certainly, Mr. Fergusson. I'll look up those figures and call you back in a few minutes."

Beside him Sheryl sighed heavily.

Chapter Seven

June 13, 2011

The final image flickered and the screen at the front of the boardroom went blank. The handful of men and women seated around the table turned their attention to Jack.

"That," Jack indicated the screen, "is the culmination of my efforts this past spring."

"Impressive." A board member swiveled his high-backed chair and steepled his fingers. "Very innovative."

Several others nodded and murmured their approval.

Jack beamed under their praise, feeling the satisfaction of success. He turned up the room lights. "Since we at Smythe-Andersson launched the Beautiful Blue line two years ago, the question has been how could we sell more product. I am pleased to report we sold over two hundred thousand units this quarter. After this little darling hits the airwaves," he gestured toward the screen where they had just watched the commercial, "those numbers will double."

Now for the dramatic pause. The presentation unfolded exactly how he had practiced. "So, gentlemen, ladies, the new question that we can begin asking ourselves is …" He made eye contact with each executive seated around the oval conference table. "What changes are needed to keep up with demand?"

A rustle of excitement swept the room and the board members broke into applause. Jack could no longer hold back a grin. He basked in his moment of glory.

Following the meeting, Jack strutted from the conference room feeling like a quarterback who had just won the Super Bowl. Throughout the office, co-workers offered their congratulations as he passed. Having a job where he was paid to be creative was rewarding. Receiving accolades and admiration for his ideas was even better.

As he reached his office door, he felt a slap on his shoulder. He turned to face his boss, George Fergusson. Fit and in his fifties, Fergusson was a hard and unforgiving taskmaster who never let the clock or the calendar dictate his work hours or those of his employees.

"Jack, you have outdone yourself this time." High praise from the man who was adept at delivering criticism in stiletto jabs. Mr. Fergusson pointed to the nameplate on Jack's office door that read Jack Baker, Director of Marketing. "If you come anywhere near those projections, I think there may be a VP position waiting for you."

"I'm shocked." Eyes wide, Jack feigned modesty. "I don't know what to say." He waved for Mr. Fergusson to follow him into his office where Jack retrieved a package from his desktop. Jack opened the envelope and with a flourish, held up the contents. "My new nameplate arrived yesterday."

With his sleeve, he buffed the shiny surface and held the plaque so his boss could read the engraved words. Jack Baker, Vice President. "And I look forward to exceeding your expectations."

"I'm sure you do." Mr. Fergusson pounded him again on the back. "Big day today, Baker. Go home and sleep in. We'll see you tomorrow, later rather than earlier."

Turning, Mr. Fergusson nearly collided with Jack's assistant. The boss frowned in annoyance. "What do you want?"

"I'm Wesley, sir. Wesley Sorg." The lanky blonde stuck out his hand. "Jack-O's co-marketing executive for the past six months."

Fergusson ignored the proffered handshake.

"If I could have just a few moments of your time." Wesley wiped his sweaty palm on his pant leg and thumped down a briefcase on Jack's desk next to the framed eight-by-ten of the Baker family on their porch at Christmas. "I'd like to show you a concept for the Beautiful Blue line that will rock your world."

Jack winced at the faux pas. There was a time and a place to address the boss and this was certainly not it.

Mr. Fergusson spoke to Wesley in clipped syllables as if speaking to a simpleton. "We already have exemplary packaging designs for Beautiful Blue. They've been on shelves for two years."

"Yes, and no offense to the amateur who designed them, but with a few very minor enhancements, we could take our look to the next level." With over-exaggerated movements, Wesley unsnapped the clasps of his case. Resembling a magician, he pulled out a stack of sketches.

Mr. Fergusson turned to Jack. "When did we hire a co-marketing executive? I didn't authorize that."

"We didn't." Jack shrugged. "He's my assistant. Just a little ambitious."

Mr. Fergusson glared at Wesley. "There are two hard, solid facts you need to know about me. I never forget a face, and I don't take kindly to people lying to me. You just dug yourself a hole, and I don't expect you'll ever climb out of it."

Mr. Fergusson turned to Jack. "Great work today, Baker."

Wesley stood slack-jawed, his cheeks red, as he watched Mr. Fergusson disappear down the hall.

"Pace yourself, kiddo." Jack slammed the lid on Wesley's briefcase. "You can't just throw designs at Mr. Fergusson. There's an opportune moment for presentations." He steered the stunned co-worker out the door. "And it's not here. And certainly not now."

Chapter Eight

June 14, 2011

Dressed in lime and tangerine pajamas, Jack wandered into the kitchen. He stretched, rubbed at his tousled hair, and scratched his stubbled cheeks. Sleeping in had felt wonderful. And he deserved it. He grinned at the memory of yesterday's triumph with the company's board of directors.

He took a box of crunchy granola from the pantry and stopped at the cupboard for a bowl. He read the note in Sheryl's neat handwriting taped to the refrigerator door. Good morning, sleepy head. I took Adam to baseball practice and the girls and I are dropping by the library. See you when we get home.

Opening the refrigerator, Jack spotted a carryout container from House of Italy. To celebrate his marketing victory yesterday evening, he had treated the family to dinner at their favorite restaurant. Reaching inside the Styrofoam box now, Jack selected a generous slice of cheese-laden pizza that he downed in three bites as he carried his bowl of cereal to the table. Dropping into a kitchen chair, he reached for the newspaper and noticed his cell phone lying on the tabletop. The message light flashed.

Spooning an oversized bite of cereal into his mouth, he opened his phone and scrolled to the text messages. Probably more congratulations from board members. Or maybe even Fergusson.

His eyebrows went up. Thirty-two unopened text messages? He pressed a couple buttons and rechecked the count. The number of messages jumped to thirty-four. He had anticipated some congratulatory notes, but this exceeded even his expectations. More than a home run, yesterday's pitch had hit the ball completely out of the park.

The home phone rang. He didn't move to answer it, preferring to hear the congratulations while he lounged in the sunny kitchen, enjoying his leisurely morning in the wake of his epic yesterday. He opened the first text message as the answering machine kicked in. "You've reached the Bakers. Please leave a message."

"Baker!" He looked up at the sound of George Fergusson's agitated voice. "Why aren't you answering your phone? They're going through everything! Get in here!"

Jack rushed to the phone. "Mr. Fergusson? What—" He heard a click. He frowned, trying to piece together reasons for Fergusson's apparent annoyance. When the dial tone clicked on, he realized he was still gripping the receiver and slowly hung the phone back in its cradle.

From outside, he heard unusual noise. Maybe Sheryl and the kids had arrived back home. But a glance at the clock told him they would still be busy with their morning schedule. Cocking his head, he listened. The strange sounds grew louder. Opening the front door, he peered outside, surprised to find the cul-de-sac jammed with parked vehicles. People were congregating on the sidewalk and in his front yard. Some had notebooks. Some carried cameras. The large cameras looked like the ones the media used.

"He's here," he heard someone say.

"Baker's at home," another called.

The crowd was not cheering congratulations. In fact, they looked serious. Like Fergusson had sounded. A man took the porch steps two at a time and shoved a microphone in Jack's face. "Mr. Baker, can you explain—"

Jack retreated inside and slammed the door. Attempting to calm his racing heart, he glanced again at his cell phone. Now there were fifty-four messages. Jack hurriedly dressed and dashed to the garage. Inside his car, he started the engine, pushed the button to open the garage door, and accelerated as soon as he could clear the elevating door. Weaving through the media cars and minivans, he was stunned to recognize the logos of local television and radio news stations as well as several newspapers.

Driving above the speed limit, he arrived at the Smythe-Andersson building and pulled into the parking lot. A parked car occupied his usual spot and all of the visitor spaces were full. Feeling like he had already run a gauntlet to escape his own driveway and neighborhood, he growled in frustration. Finally, Jack found a parking place down the block and strode to the Smythe-Andersson building.

Inside the office, a number of strangers poured through files. Fellow employees milled about, talking in whispers, looking troubled.

Red-faced, eyes bulging, and appearing to be on the verge of a stroke, George Fergusson exploded out of his office. "Jack, where have you been? We've been trying to reach you all morning!"

"I came as soon as I could. What's going on?"

Mr. Fergusson grabbed Jack by the arm and pulled him into his office, shutting the door firmly behind them.

"We have a grave situation." He turned to his desk and picked up a document. "Is that your signature?"

Jack glanced at the paper. The mark scrawled there was as undecipherable as a doctor's signature. "No."

Mr. Fergusson shook his head and moved closer. "Let me ask you again. Is that your signature?" He was practically nose-to-nose with Jack, sending some nonverbal signal that Jack didn't understand.

Jack hesitated and repeated, "No."

Mr. Fergusson raised his eyebrows.

Jack tried again. "Yes?"

Nodding, Mr. Fergusson sat in his chair and sighed. "Well, then I regret to tell you that you signed off on a label with a critical misprint."

"Signed off?" This time Jack's eyebrows shot up. "What are you talking about?"

His boss handed him a bottle and pointed to the label. "Use in a well-ventilated area," he read aloud. "Press down on cap and twist to open. Do now inhale fumes." He looked at Jack and repeated the last instruction. "Do now inhale."

Jack frowned and took the bottle. Squinting, he read the label himself. "That can't be right." He reread it. Shaking his head, he looked at Mr. Fergusson. "Does anyone actually read these instructions?"

"Apparently, they follow them. Over 200 mindless drones have been hospitalized since these bottles shipped last Thursday. Last night, the Environmental Protection Agency tied all the illnesses to us."

"I never signed off on anything."

"No, you haven't."

Jack indicated the paper on his boss's desk. "Sir, I've never seen that form in my life."

Mr. Fergusson tossed the form to the other side of his desk. "Because we've never used them. And believe you me, someone's going to lose their job over that one but here's the real problem." He leaned forward and rested his elbows on the desk. "Without this form, and your signature on it, they'll shut us down."

Jack caught his breath. "Are you throwing me to the wolves?"

"Hundreds of jobs will be lost. In this economy, our town of Wooded Falls may not recover for years. If ever."

"Unless?"

Mr. Fergusson came around the desk and put his arm about Jack's shoulders. He spoke softly. "It's for the good of the company, son. I know that's always been your top priority."

Jack shifted his weight and stuffed fists into his pockets. "Are you asking me to take one for the Gipper?"

The company owner patted Jack's shoulder. "If you take the hit, only one job will be lost. I'll bring you back with a handsome raise as soon as all of this blows over."

Jack swallowed and tugged at his collar. "Sir, I'm not comfortable with this at all. I have a family. And a house I can barely afford. I'm our only source of income. This could really hurt us."

Mr. Fergusson stepped back. "I'm not asking if you're comfortable with it." From under bushy eyebrows, hard eyes bored into Jack's. "The report has been filed. They're waiting to speak with you. The question is, are you going to be a team player and save hundreds of jobs, or are you going to make this messy for everyone?"

There was a sharp knock on the office door and Mr. Fergusson's assistant stuck in her head. "Jack, the investigator wants to talk to you."

Jack looked at his boss with raised eyebrows. Mr. Fergusson nodded toward the door and then turned away.

Chapter Nine

Sitting across the kitchen table from her husband that evening, Sheryl knotted her hands in her lap. The usual music in the house was absent. Even the children had retreated to their rooms.

"Fired?" She repeated the foreign sounding word.

Jack slouched and the chair creaked. "Yep."

For several more minutes, they sat in silence while outside the kitchen window birds twittered and sang as if the Baker's entire world had not just come crashing down.

"Okay." Sheryl shifted gears. "We need a plan."

"Yep."

She brightened. "Do you have one?"

"One what?"

"A plan." She tapped her finger on the tabletop. "Do you have a plan?"

Jack sighed. "I'm still letting this news sink in."

The timer buzzed, and she stood. As she opened the oven, the cozy smell of baked lasagna flooded the room, and she folded the foil off the baking dish. Her hands mittened in thick potholders, she slid the hot pan back inside to brown the cheese and closed the oven door, suddenly aware she felt too upset to think about eating. Glancing at Jack's solemn face, she suspected this turn of events had dampened his appetite as well.

Back at the table, she placed her hand over his. "Giving things some time is probably a good idea. This is a pretty big shock. We have enough money in the bank to make the mortgage payment on Friday."

Jack remained silent.

"Of course, most of the utilities would have been paid out of your next paycheck."

Her husband stared at the tabletop.

"And your car payment." She heard panic creep into her voice. "The insurance bill will come soon, and the down payment for Adam's braces is due next week, and Adam and Michelle need clothes to start school." As the list grew her voice rose in pitch. "And don't forget the credit cards."

Jack slid his hand out from under hers. She noticed indents where her nails had pressed into his skin.

She took a deep breath to calm herself. "I'm sorry, Jack. I understand that you need time to think."

She reached across the table and lifted his chin until his eyes met hers. "We're in this together. I'll help you anyway I can." He started to pull away, but she cupped his face in her palms. "But Jack, please hear me. We can't just think too long. We can't afford it."

Chapter Ten

Thursday, June 16, 2011

Sheryl put the mayonnaise back into the refrigerator and added a napkin to the tray that held a thick roast beef sandwich. Lettuce and tomato, no pickle. Taking a deep breath, she plastered on a smile and carefully balanced the tray so the iced tea didn't spill.

In the Man Cave, their special name for the lower level family room, Sheryl set the lunch on an end table next to Jack's recliner. "Here you are, dear."

Jack stared blankly at the television.

Glancing at the screen, she frowned. "Does watching infomercials help you think?"

His eyes still on the TV, Jack took a bite of his sandwich.

She went to the sliding glass door and pulled open the drapes. Even in the middle of the day, this room where the family often gathered did resemble a cave with the sun tightly shut out. The cheery light was a welcome addition, and Sheryl opened the door to let in fresh air through the screen. "I have an idea. Do you want to hear it?"

Jack squinted at the sunlight and took another bite.

Hands on her hips, Sheryl stepped in front of the TV screen. "Jack, for two days you have barely communicated."

He grunted, trying to peer around her to see the flickering images.

"Unless, of course, you consider primitive grunting some way of talking to your wife. But since you're not Tarzan and I'm not Jane, let's use multi-syllable words."

His eyes met hers.

She smiled. "There you are." She sat down next to him. "Any thoughts on what we can do next?"

He reached for his glass. "Nope."

"I have an idea." Sheryl spun her wedding ring on her finger. "I could look into what it would take for me to go back to teaching."

"Absolutely not." He sat up straighter. "Kim has come so far, made good progress since she arrived. She needs a mommy. You are needed here."

Sheryl nodded. "You're right, of course. I was also thinking—" She reached for his hand, but he picked up the remote, turned up the volume, and once more turned his full attention to the infomercial channel.

Chapter Eleven

MONDAY, JUNE 27, 2011

Two weeks later, Jack sat in his home office determined to make this the day he launched off dead center and made progress in life. He felt responsible for his family. There was the payment for Adam's braces to cover, school clothes to buy, and the credit cards to keep up. And even though this month's house payment had been paid, in mere weeks, next month's installment would be due.

Day after day, his cell phone remained silent as a tomb. He frequently scrolled for messages. Nothing. Texts? Nada. The small device may as well have weighed a thousand pounds. Fergusson had said he would bring Jack back to Smythe-Andersson as soon as the public outrage around the misspelling on the label quieted down. Sitting in his home office, Jack felt like a prisoner marking days on the cell wall—noting each day Fergusson didn't call. Jack had done nothing in weeks. Days piled together like a living death and lately he'd been behaving like a zombie. Just ask Sheryl.

He heard his wife humming in the kitchen and the tune grew louder as she came down the hall. Peering around the corner of his office door, she looked sweet and cheerful. And abundantly patient.

"Are you formulating a plan in here?" She looked questioningly at the phone in his hand.

"It never rings anymore."

She studied him.

"I had no idea how much I enjoyed being needed." The enormity of the bleakness of his current situation overwhelmed him, and he swung his chair away from the sympathy in Sheryl's eyes. He couldn't stand it.

He felt her hand squeeze his shoulder. Moments later he heard her leave the room. Her footsteps were soft as she returned to the kitchen. Her humming had ceased.

Chapter Twelve

Monday, August 8, 2011

Sheryl crossed the lawn to the mailbox. The grass wilted in the late summer heat but to save on the water bill, she had not turned on the sprinklers. She doubted Jack even noticed what the landscape looked like these days, though previously he had been keen to keep a yard with strong curb appeal.

Getting the mail used to be fun. A highlight of her day. She sorted through the ads for shopping deals, marked invitations on her calendar, and put the bills into the budget folder. These days, she dreaded the daily visit from the mailman. Bills came in droves. While she had never even seen an overdue notice before, now she had a collection of them. Though reluctant to retrieve the daily delivery, she refused to leave the bills together in the mailbox where they appeared to multiply.

She paused to check on Michelle. Sitting on the neighbor's porch with her best friend, her daughter's head was bent over the board game they were playing.

I love this neighborhood.

Noting the bushes lining the sidewalk needed a trim, and weeds were sprouting in the flowerbed mulch, she hurried up the porch steps and into the house. She had cancelled the twice-monthly yard service for the time being.

She was surprised to see Jack's office chair empty. Standing at the top of the stairs, she didn't hear the sound of the TV coming from the Man Cave either. Hope stirred. Maybe today he would get his act together.

She checked the bedroom. No Jack.

She found him sitting at the kitchen table. In a robe and disheveled pajamas, he stared at a newspaper. A scrubby beard shadowed his face below his unkempt hair. For nearly a minute, she watched. His eyes didn't move. He didn't turn a page. He's not even reading it.

Sheryl plopped the bills beside him on the table. "Four more bills today. We're past due on three credit cards, the mortgage, cell phones, and the cable." She sat beside him. "Any thoughts on how we're going to get caught up?"

She clenched and unclenched her hands under the table as she waited for his answer.

Jack shook his head. "Nothing's coming to me. Let me do some more thinking on it."

Sheryl looked out the window. Outside, Adam and his friend kicked a soccer ball around in the backyard. The strains of Kim Possible came from the TV in the living room where Kimmy watched her favorite program. She patted the bills as she rose to leave the room. "Okay. I'll just leave these here for you."

Chapter Thirteen

Wednesday, August 10, 2011

Sheryl glanced up from slicing vegetables for stir-fry to see Kim come into the kitchen rubbing her eyes and dragging her stuffed koala bear by a round ear.

"Well, look who's up from her nap. Want some milk?"

She nodded, and Sheryl pulled the milk carton from the refrigerator. She lifted Kim onto the counter and watched her daughter drink. How in the world are we going to take care of these precious children? Sheryl and Jack had already agreed to postpone shopping for school clothes, but real fear swept over her as she prayed they would continue to be able to feed everyone. Surely the situation would not get that bad. Jack's next job must be just around the corner.

When Kim handed back the glass, Sheryl laughed at her milk mustache. Singing a children's song, she dabbed Kim's face and swung the little girl down from the countertop.

Through the kitchen windows, Sheryl saw Adam and Michelle playing in the backyard and knew they would soon be clamoring for their mid-afternoon snack. She set out crackers, cheese, and lemonade. Kim called from the living room, and Sheryl changed the TV channel according to her plea. On her way back to the kitchen, she passed the master bedroom. Pausing, she leaned her head against the closed door. No sound came from within. Fighting tears, she lifted her chin and opened the door.

The room was dark, but she could see a large lump on Jack's side of the bed. She went to the window shade and pulled the cord, flooding the room with afternoon sunshine.

"Sweetie?" There was no response. "It's three o'clock. Are you getting out of bed today?"

The lump didn't move.

"Sweetie?"

The lump groaned.

She rocked the mass. "Jack?"

He groaned. "Not right now. Maybe in a few minutes." He rolled away from her and stretched the covers snug around his ears.

"I see." Biting her lip, Sheryl left the room. Back in the breezy kitchen, she circled the room three times, then went to the freezer.

Storming back into their bedroom, she yanked the blankets from the bed.

"Hey!" Jack rolled over and squinted at her, his hand shading his eyes.

In one swift move, she emptied a pitcher of ice water squarely on his head.

"Aahhh!" Sputtering and spitting, he gasped and bolted up. Now his eyes were wide open and he clutched at ice chips that slipped down the front of his pajamas.

Sheryl straddled her wet husband and grabbed his shirt by the collar. She pulled him toward her until they were eye to eye.

"Now you listen to me, Jack Baker, and you listen good." She emphasized each staccato word with a shake. "You've been dealt a bad hand, there's no denying it. But I am not going to let you lie around and sulk anymore. Do you understand?"

He stared wide-eyed at his wife.

"You have too much talent to be wasting away like this. You are the best marketing executive I've ever seen, and there are a hundred companies out there who would kill to have someone like you on their team. Now, it's time to figure out who they are. You got it?" She let him drop back down onto his soggy, frigid pillow. "Now get out of bed. We're going job hunting."

Chapter Fourteen

Dry and dressed after Sheryl's drenching, Jack lined up a legal size notepad and two pens on his home office desk. Showered, shaved, and dressed in clean jeans and a polo shirt, he swiveled his chair to face the computer.

He took a deep breath and entered "sales" and "Wooded Falls" into the internet search window. Two hundred and thirty-two results. He nodded in satisfaction. A good pond in which to fish.

"Door-to-door vacuum cleaner salesman." Gag. They still do that? Go to the store, people. No door-to-door sales for me.

He clicked on the next opportunity. "Zubba, zubba, zimma … Big John's Auto Sales." Uh, no thank you. He chuckled at the thought of Jack Baker hawking cars for the cheesy, flashy dealership owner on TV.

His sense of satisfaction gradually leaked away as he worked through the columns of opportunities. With less enthusiasm, he clicked another listing.

"Pizza sales reps needed?" He snorted. "That's not sales. That's taking orders." He rubbed his temples. "Are there no interesting jobs in this town?"

He heard Sheryl humming her way down the hall. She brought a large glass of lemonade.

Jack eyed his wife and the full glass. "You're not going to dump that on me, are you?"

She set the glass on his desk. "Don't tempt me." Leaning over his shoulder, she read the screen. "What have we found?"

Jack took a sip of the lemonade and smacked his lips. "Zippo."

He set down the drink and swiveled his chair to face Sheryl who had settled into the wingback chair. "There's not a single job on here worth doing." He gestured toward the monitor. "It's disgusting. 'Sales managers needed for exciting new opportunity.' They don't even tell you what you're selling. And look, there's a $225 fee to apply. What is this, some kind of help wanted internet scam? I'm here because I need to make money—not throw dollars away. It's ridiculous."

"Hmm, sounds like there's not a single job here that you're interested in."

"Bingo." He paused to smile his appreciation for his wife's obvious understanding. She had beautiful blue eyes.

"So that's out." She cocked her head to the side. "Are there any jobs that offer a paycheck?"

As comprehension dawned, Jack marveled at the woman before him. "You stinker," he retorted without anger.

He turned back to the monitor and started once more down the list. "I suppose."

Sheryl moved behind him and placed her arms gently on his shoulders. "Okay, then let's focus on those for now and we'll keep our eyes open for the interesting ones as they become available. Sound good?"

Jack resisted grinning at his wife's simple, yet profound wisdom. "I'm not entirely sure I appreciate your wit right now."

She squeezed his shoulders. "Too bad, because I've got lots more." She was smiling as she turned to leave but Jack got the last word as he lovingly patted her on the backside.

"This is a pessimism room. Happy, rosy, sunshiny people meet three doors down on the right."

"I love you." She left, humming.

His eyes on the screen, he murmured, "Yeah, get out of here. If you loved me, you'd sulk with me. Crazy, levelheaded woman."

Jack spent the next hour studying job descriptions and taking notes. Rolling his chair back from the desk, he rubbed his head and fumed. Minimum wage? Where are the jobs for people who are trying to support a family? Returning to the monitor one more time, he finally spotted an ad that glimmered with hope. "Unlimited potential for the right sales rep. Click for details."

"Unlimited potential? That sounds a little more like it. So, what's the job?" Clicking on the link, he exhaled. "Come on now, Daddy needs a cool job."

He grimaced when the giant face of Big John of Big John's Used Cars appeared larger than life size on the screen. "Big John's Auto? Really? No wonder the job pays so well—it's dirty money."

He paused as he remembered Sheryl's gentle question, "Are there any jobs that offer a paycheck?"

He fiercely shook his head. "I can't work there. I won't. He's unethical. This is not going to happen. End of story."

Chapter Fifteen

AUGUST 11, 2011

The next morning, Jack found himself across the desk from Big John. In an extra-extra-large flannel shirt, the middle-aged man chewed a toothpick while he scrutinized Jack's résumé.

What was taking the guy so long? Jack's résumé was flawless, and Big John should be turning cartwheels.

Finally, Big John looked up. "I don't think I can use ya."

Jack blinked. "I'm sorry, huh?"

"Well, you dun a lot of sellin' and what not, but you ain't never worked in the car business, per say." He threw his toothpick in the trashcan and pulled another one from his desk. "We ain't sellin' eight dollar bottles of floor scrub. We're selling two thousand pound killin' machines what helps people get to work and all. It's the second biggest investment folks ever make. Now that's an important job there."

Big John pushed away from his desk and heaved himself to his feet. "People don't like your cleaners, they just pitch 'em. You can't do that with yer automobile. Besides, ain't you that guy in the paper who poisoned all them kids?" He shook his big jowled head. "I don't want you givin' my lot a bad name."

Jack experienced a wave of incredulity followed by an even larger sense of rage. He drew himself up. "Your name has been banned from public schools as profanity. How could I make your reputation worse?"

Big John calmly waved his hand as if shooing away an unpleasant odor. "That ain't official yet, and besides, my reputation ain't all bad. If it is, why do folks keep coming in?" He raised his eyebrows and looked to Jack for an answer.

Jack leaped to his feet. "Because you're the only dealership within thirty miles of Wooded Falls."

"Well, then they ought to thank me for not packing up and moving to a more grateful community." He paused and looked deep in thought. "Hey, I ought a use that in my next commercial."

"You're a crook." Halfway to the door, Jack whirled around for a final volley. "You sold a woman a car that needed to be push-started."

"Hey now, I gave that lady a deal." Pointing the toothpick, he poked the air like he was deflating a balloon. "I knocked fifty bucks off the window price."

"She was an eighty-three-year-old widow. With a walker." Jack gestured to the large, framed newspaper story on the wall. "Then you had the gall to have the article matted and framed." In the photo, the frail old woman was nearly crying while Big John grinned enthusiastically and gave a thumbs up to the photographer. Probably the same photojournalist who had taken the photo of the Baker house decorated for Christmas each year.

Big John puffed out his barrel chest. "That was a big win for me. Let's see you make that sale, cleaner man."

"This is ridiculous." Jack went to the door, turned and fired back. "I don't know why I came. I wouldn't work for you if this were the only job in Wooded Falls."

Big John rolled his toothpick to the side of his mouth. "You're stormin' out like you're refusing an offer or somethin'. I turned you away, remember? Nobody in town is gonna hire you. You're probably gonna have to move out of the county to get a job. Maybe out of the state."

"Oh, I'll find a job, don't you lose a minute of sleep over that. I'm not moving anywhere." He pointed to the news photo of the elderly woman. "Wooded Falls actually means something to me, and this is where I'm raising my family. I've worked my whole life to build a good reputation in this community. It's going to take a lot more that some newspaper story to destroy it."

Chapter Sixteen

Sheryl prepared supper, occasionally glancing at the late afternoon TV talk show. Jack tramped in and flopped into a kitchen chair. Resting his head in his hands, he looked like a tire that had suddenly gone flat.

She quickly washed her hands and went over to rub his shoulders. As Jack's retelling of his interview ended, her hands grew still. "He thought you'd give Big John's a bad name?"

Jack laughed ruefully. "My first job interview in twenty-five years and the biggest swindler in town accused me of having a bad reputation."

She started to massage his shoulders again, noting the tenseness he carried there. "That's okay. There are hundreds of other places to work in Wooded Falls. We'll just apply somewhere else. Getting a job can't be that hard."

From the television in the living room, the introduction to the early edition of the local news played. In the tease at the beginning of the program, Smythe-Andersson headlined. Sheryl's hands froze. Jack cocked his head to listen.

They moved to the living room love seat and suffered through the commercials until the news anchor launched into the lead story. Sheryl gasped at the picture of Jack that filled the screen. He looked menacing. Like a gangster.

"Where did they find such a nasty photo?" She reached for his hand.

The newsman reported, "Tonight, learn more about the negative impact that one man, Jack Baker, had on Wooded Falls's most prestigious company—an impact that nearly closed the plant's doors and could have cost the community as many as two hundred forty jobs."

A video bite showed a dignified Mr. Fergusson, looking very much the victim. "We told him to stress the need for appropriate breathing apparatus in his marketing, but he always had to do things his own way. He was stubborn. We had no idea what kind of negative ripple effects his actions would cause." Mr. Fergusson looked directly into the camera. "We want to apologize to the families who have been affected by this. You'll be happy to know we have taken a proactive approach and are now developing all-natural, environmentally friendly cleaning solutions. We're calling the new line Good for Us."

The camera cut back to the news anchor with the ugly photo of Jack in the background. "All this and more, tonight at seven, nine, ten, and eleven with replays tomorrow morning at five, six, seven, and noon on channel nine—Wooded Falls's most watched news network."

Chapter Seventeen

Sunday, October 23, 2011

Jack helped Kim into her sweater and looked at his family. They looked good. Well groomed. Prosperous. They didn't look like the children of a father who had spent the last four months being turned down for minimum wage jobs.

"Okay, everyone into the van." He pointed to the garage. "We don't want to be late for church."

During the drive, Jack and Sheryl talked about the weather. They talked about lunch plans. They talked about upcoming parent teacher meetings. They did not talk about what was on both of their hearts. They never talked about Jack's job loss or bills or their economic future in front of the children. They had agreed early on not to burden the young ones with their adult worries.

Arriving at church, Sheryl greeted her friends. Jack put on his winning smile, offering a hearty handshake and a back slap for his buddies. Following his family though the open door of the church, a greeter Jack had not seen before welcomed him.

"Good morning." The older gentleman's handshake was warm and firm. "And how are you, good sir?"

There was something familiar about the kind face. Jack shook his hand and offered a customary smile. "Great, thanks. How are you?"

The small, elderly man looked like he had weathered the storms of life and survived them well. "Aw, I can't complain. Not one bit."

Jack nodded and tried to move away, but the greeter placed a hand on his shoulder. "Can I be praying for you about anything?"

For a moment, Jack felt like telling the stranger of the challenge he was facing. Then he saw the people grouping around them. He didn't want to cause a scene. He would be happy enough to slog through the church routine and get back home in time for football.

He swallowed back his near confession. "No, I'm fine. Thanks though."

As he moved through the hallway, he thought he could feel the man's sad eyes following him. "I'm fine," he repeated to himself. "I'm fine."

Chapter Eighteen

Monday, October 24, 2011

Sheryl wiped Kim's face and hands. "Okay, honey. You can go play now." She cleared Kim's dishes as Michelle got up from the breakfast table.

"Put your bowl in the sink," Sheryl mechanically corrected.

"Sure, Mom." Michelle obediently followed instructions and gathered her schoolbooks.

Adam hurried into the kitchen, opened the pantry door and quickly selected his favorite cereal.

"Busy day at school?"

"Uh-huh." Adam poured his cereal. Setting a gallon of milk on the counter, he knocked over a stack of mail. The envelopes cascaded to the floor like spilled milk. Adam groaned and leaned over to pick them up.

Sheryl waved away his efforts. "Don't worry about it. I'll take care of them. You eat so you don't miss the bus." She scooped up the envelopes, desperately wishing she really could take care of them. She felt the stress mount as she sat down at the table with the stack of unopened bills.

The phone rang. Adam picked up the receiver. "Hello?" He paused, listening. "Yeah, she's right here." He brought the phone to Sheryl. "Mom, it's for you."

"Hello?" She answered in her cheery phone voice. Adam returned to his seat and shoveled a spoonful of cereal into his mouth. "I'm sorry, who is this?" She frowned and glanced at Adam.

"Who is it?" Adam's spoon stopped halfway to the bowl.

She pointed to the doorway and mouthed, "Go."

He raised his eyebrows and mouthed, "I'm eating."

"Excuse me just a minute," she said into the phone and covered the mouthpiece. "Sweetie, why don't you go downstairs and watch TV?"

"Before school?" He sounded incredulous. "I'm eating. What do they want?"

"You can finish your cereal later." She used her tough mom tone and nodded toward the other room.

He looked longingly at his cereal. "Aw, I don't do soggy cereal."

"Adam." She escalated to her absolutely-no-nonsense tone. "You can pour a new bowl when I'm finished."

He looked up, quickly reading her mood based on past experience.

"On second thought, take your cereal with you. You can eat downstairs." She pointed his way out. "Now go."

Grumbling, Adam left the table. "Fine. Attack the visible one."

As Adam left the room, Sheryl returned to the caller. "Sorry about that. Yes … yes, I understand that we've fallen a little behind … Two months? Are you sure?" She did the math in her head. "Yes, that sounds right."

She tried to collect her thoughts and speak clearly. "We've experienced a financial crisis but intend to get everything caught up as soon as we can. It's just going to take some time."

She straightened the pile of bills as she spoke. "See, my husband lost his job, and we've had no income for quite some time. Our savings are wiped out, and he hasn't had any luck finding a new job. We're not sure what we're going to do, but we're trying—"

She paused at the interruption.

"What? Uh, no, I'm not able to make a payment of $212.16. Did you hear what I just said? My husband is out of work. Now, I can assure you that we're not the kind of people that you typically deal with. We're experiencing a temporary hiccup. We have always paid our bills on time, and we will pay you as soon as we can—" Again she was interrupted. She felt frustration rising. Are they listening to me at all?

"No, I'm not able to make a payment of $212.16. Normally, I could and I would, but we just don't have the money right now. This is a situation that I have never been in before, and I can tell you—"

She rolled her eyes in exasperation. "Well, then you're going to have to add the late fee because I don't have the money right now." What more could she say?

"Well, now why would you do that? I just told you that we'll pay you as soon as we have the money. What does that mean, turn me over to a collection agency? No, I … if you would listen to me … listen! I need a little more time."

She rested her forehead in her hand. How much more time did she need? How much longer would this desolate season go on? When would the Baker family get back to normal?

Chapter Nineteen

That night Sheryl lay in bed, staring at the ceiling. Feeling emotionally imprisoned by the morning's phone call, she stretched her arm to Jack's empty side of the bed. He was still in front of the home computer, searching for jobs. When she finally heard his steps coming down the hall, she prayed for good news.

But she didn't have to ask. Even in the dark, she could feel discouragement and lethargy in his movements as he entered the room, changed for bed, and climbed in beside her.

She reached for his hand and squeezed it. "Any luck?"

"Nothing that pays well."

"I don't care what you do or how much you make at this point; we just need you to start making money again."

"Whoa, what's wrong?"

Perhaps her attempts to protect him from the realities of life in the Baker household had backfired. She wanted to stay respectful but the humiliation of the morning's call burned in her soul. She ached to scream at him about her pain.

She pressed back panic and spoke gently. "I got a call from Banner Card today."

"Okay?"

"I was made to feel like some third-rate citizen because we've fallen behind in our payments. He was rude, he was mean, he threatened me—"

Jack bolted to a sitting position. "He threatened you?"

Sheryl could hear fierce protectiveness in his voice. She continued. "He threatened to turn me over to a collection agency if I didn't pay him $200. They will sue us to get the money if we don't pay within ten days."

Jack flopped back on his pillow. "Sue us? For what? We don't have anything to take."

"Our cars? Our furniture? I don't know. I've never been sued before." She took a breath. "This is new to me, Jack, and I'm not enjoying it."

He touched her shoulder. She knew he could feel her shaking. "Oh, hon." He pulled her close and wrapped his arms around her. Held in his protective embrace she allowed hot tears to flow.

"I don't like being poor, Jack," she said between quiet sobs.

"We're not poor."

"We're not rich. We're not even middle class. Middle class people pay their bills on time and don't get sued by credit card companies."

She felt him stiffen but he didn't push her away. At least not physically.

He sounded overly patient as he responded. "I'm doing the best that I can, all right? I haven't applied for a job in twenty-five years. It's harder than you think. The job descriptions are all gibberish. I need an interpreter to decode them."

She knew what he wasn't saying. After the Smythe-Andersson debacle everyone in the community thinks I'm practically a criminal.

Sheryl slipped from his arms and rolled onto her own pillow. Her words sounded hollow as she stated the simple truth. "We have six more credit cards and we're just as far behind on those. If this is the best you can do, we may lose everything." She knew she was hurting him but she had to share her desperation. She felt a shiver of fear as she heard Jack's sigh.

Chapter Twenty

Tuesday, October 25, 2011

George Fergusson sat at the large, oval table with the other executives listening as the latest in a string of replacements for Jack Baker pitched his strategy for the Good for Us line. His name was Melvin something-or-other and he had an impressive résumé. He was twenty-four years old and supposedly a marketing wonder.

But he looked like a nervous wreck. His voice shook, and two deep sweat rings marked the shirt underneath his armpits. He pointed at a drawing of a rugged trailblazer who was chipping away brush with a machete with one hand, and holding a can of Good for Us floor cleaner in the other. Fergusson turned away in disgust.

Melvin continued. "So, um, the idea is that we're now offering all-natural cleaning solutions. This is revolutionary. I mean, nobody else anywhere is doing what we are doing so we're going to focus on being the trailblazers. This gives us a competitive edge because people always stay loyal to the companies that are first to hit the market with a product."

Fergusson sighed. He missed Baker. In frustration, he barked, "Not true."

Melvin froze, eyes wide.

Fergusson cleared his throat and continued. "Can you back that up with facts?"

The man spit and sputtered as he rummaged through a pile of paperwork.

Fergusson thumped the table with his fist. "My seven-year-old granddaughter could disprove that theory with one hand and an internet connection. Where did you gather that information?"

"I, I … wh … um … think of Coke?"

"Are you making this up?" Fergusson narrowed his eyes. "Even if that concept was accurate—and it isn't—your idea would only work against us. We're not the first green cleaning company."

Melvin swallowed hard, his sweat rings growing larger. "But I … I was told that this was brand new. That we were starting something totally different."

"Brand new for us, you moron. Did you research our competition at all before developing this campaign or did you just pull this out of your armpit?"

"Wh … um, like … what do you mean?"

Fergusson stood and gathered his papers. The other executives quickly followed his example.

"Gentlemen, this meeting is over." He turned to his crumpling marketing director.

Melvin suddenly looked hopeful. "Yes, sir?"

"If I ever lock eyes with you on this property again, I will personally wring you out and make you drink your own sweat, do you understand me?"

Melvin gasped. "Yes, sir."

The executives cleared a path as their boss strode from the boardroom.

As Fergusson stormed down the hall, his young assistant, Miranda, clipped along on her very high heels, notebook in hand, trying to keep up. The peroxide blond, team sales manager, Jen, followed in his wake.

"When I said replace Baker, I didn't mean with a corpse." Fergusson hooked a thumb back towards the room where he had just abandoned the whimpering Melvin. "What about the other applicants?"

Miranda scanned the column in her notebook. Every name except one had a line through it. She crossed out Melvin's name. "Actually, of the fifty-seven we interviewed, he was the most qualified."

Fergusson stopped and stared at her.

"Turns out, a good marketing mind can be somewhat difficult to come by." She tapped the list with a manicured fingertip. "Probably why Puriease has been trying to steal Jack away from us for years."

"Right." Fergusson snorted. "Good thing he was so dedicated to us. If they had gotten him, we'd all be flipping chicken patties right now."

He saw Miranda look at Jen, who hesitated.

"What?"

"That's the thing." Jen shifted her weight. "Apparently, our new sales guy, Jim, was talking with a Puriease rep at the Colorado convention last week, and he may have accidentally mentioned Jack's departure."

"Are you telling me that Puriease knows Jack is on the market?"

"Yes, sir."

He turned to Miranda and pointed back to the boardroom. "And you're telling me that schmuck is our most qualified replacement?"

Miranda nodded. "That appears to be the case."

Fergusson planted his hands on his hips. "This could end badly for us. We need a plan. We've got to make sure Puriease never gets their hands on Jack Baker."

Chapter Twenty-one

On the front porch, Sheryl sat in the rocking chair but wasn't rocking. Just last Christmas, the Baker family had posed on this very porch, richly adorned for the Christmas holiday season. So much had changed for them in such a rapid time.

Tonight, the distant streetlight cast a soft glow, illuminating the gently swaying crab apple trees. She looked at the empty rocking chair beside her. She and Jack used to sit out here in the quiet moments after the kids were in bed. They hadn't shared the evening ritual for a long time.

Jack wasn't home yet from his latest attempt at a job interview. She didn't know if she should consider that good or bad. Maybe he'd gotten a job and they were busy working out the details. Maybe he stopped to buy something to celebrate.

Finally, he drove up the driveway and she heard the garage door open and close. Sheryl prayed for good news.

In a few moments, he came out the front door. She didn't have to ask how his day had gone. Even in the dim light, she could see he was disheartened in the way he walked. And in the way he didn't pick her up and swing her around with the good news that he was once more gainfully employed. Her heart sank.

"What a day." He collapsed into the other chair. "I'm starting to think it's going to be impossible to get a good job around here."

She bristled. "You don't need a good job, Jack. You just need an income." She was surprised at the venom and volume in her voice.

"Whoa, I don't deserve that." He gestured toward the house where the children slept soundly. "I've already had a very long day."

"With nothing to show for it. So what good is it?" She quickly looked to the neighbor's home. Had they heard? "You might as well have been here, helping me with the kids. At least you'd be accomplishing something."

He inhaled deeply and she heard his frustration.

His voice was tight when he finally spoke. "I love you, Sheryl. I love you to pieces, but you can't just tear into me like that." He rocked forward and planted his hands on his knees. "This is how we used to talk to each other, remember? Back when neither one of us thought we were going to make our marriage work. I don't want to go back there. I really don't. The verbal boxing gloves need to stay retired." He put a hand on the arm of her chair. "You've got to understand I'm fighting a few emotions myself."

She choked back tears. "Well, you're sure hiding it well."

He started rocking. "What do you want me to do, Sheryl? You want me to walk around mad at the world? Slam a few doors? Kick the neighbor's dog? Would that make you feel better?"

"I need you to show me that you're at least a little worried. That this isn't some big joke to you and that you're going to fix it."

He rocked faster. "That's what you want to hear? That I'm worried? Fine. I'm worried. I'm worried that the secure life I've spent fifteen years building for us might actually be so fragile that a few bad months could completely wipe out everything." Though hushed, his voice was intense with passion. "Every time I'm rejected by a minimum wage job, I'm worried that maybe I'm not as valuable as I thought I was."

He burst from his chair and paced across the porch. "I'm worried that unless Mr. Fergusson keeps his word and takes me back, I'm not going to be able to provide the kind of life that I've always wanted to give to the woman and children that I love." He stopped and faced her. "I'm worried that for the first time in my life, I've got a problem, and it's not within my power to fix it." Looking broken and miserable, he leaned against a broad porch column.

Sheryl came to Jack, tears wet on her cheeks. "You are the most valuable person in the world to me, with or without a job. Don't ever get confused about that." She put her arms around his neck. "But I think it is within your power to fix our problem. You are the most creative man I've ever met. Don't just fill out an application and walk away. Use that creativity to set yourself apart."

Jack's eyebrows rose and he stared off into the night. She heard him murmur. "Use creativity to get a new job." Even in the dimness, Sheryl could see the glint of a new light in his eyes.

Chapter Twenty-two

Thursday, October 27, 2011

Jack carefully timed his entrance to Arctic Artie's after the breakfast rush and before the lunch crowd arrived. He had already been turned down for this job but desperation drove him back.

He approached the cashier, a slender teen with her hair drawn back into a sleek ponytail. She responded with a friendly smile, her hand poised over the register. "Hi, can I take your order?"

"Can I speak with Eddie?"

Her hand dropped as she called to the back. "Eddie, there's a man here to see you."

In a few moments the young manager came to the counter. "Yes, sir. I am the manager of Arctic Artie's. You wanted to see me?"

Jack tried to sound positive, confident. "I filled out an application a few days ago. I wanted to check in and see if you've made a decision on that position yet."

"Not yet," the manager said. "Still looking."

"Okay, well, I wanted to make you aware of the fact I am very interested in the position. I've been out of work for a long time and I have three kids to feed. With Christmas just around the corner, I need to start making some money."

Eddie nodded. "Duly noted, thanks." The man turned back to the kitchen.

Jack felt desperation rise. "Could you please give my application a second look? I'm extremely motivated to give this company my best."

Eddie came around the end of the counter, put his arm around Jack's shoulders and walked him out of hearing range of his employees.

"Look, I'm sure you're a great guy, and I bet you can flip a patty as well as anyone here but the truth of the matter is … you're just not my type." Eddie nodded over his shoulder toward the kitchen.

As Jack looked at the employees gathered there, comprehension dawned. Every one of the employees was a pretty young woman.

Eddie leaned closer and confided, "In high school, the hotties ignored me. Now they sweep the floors I walk on. You understand, right? Sure you do." Eddie squeezed Jack's shoulder and turned back to the kitchen.

As a last ditch effort, Jack called out, "I'll work for free."

Eddie halted and turned back. "There's an interesting concept." He slowly took a step toward Jack. "How's that?"

Jack was making this up as he went along. Reaching back to his keen marketing skills, he crafted a plan on the spot. "I'll work the first week for free. If you like the way I work, cut me a check. If not, I'll walk and you can keep my pay for yourself. Call this a risk-free trial."

Eddie's eyes narrowed in thought and Jack could tell he was intrigued by the unique concept. "So, if I decide to fire you after the first week, I get to keep your pay?"

Jack swallowed "No questions asked."

"Risk-free trial, huh? That's original. I like that." The manager studied him. "You should be a marketing guy or something."

If you only knew.

Eddie clapped his hands and returned to his work behind the counter. "Be here at noon tomorrow."

Chapter Twenty-three

FRIDAY, OCTOBER 28, 2011

Outside the bathroom door, Jack could hear the din of the noon crowd of patrons, while inside the bathroom, he stared at his reflection in the mirror. Maybe this was Eddie's test to see if he could pocket Jack's first week paycheck. Jack looked ridiculous in the Arctic Artie's penguin mascot costume. He resembled an oversized, out-of-place, non-flight bird.

As if to confirm his thoughts, a tough looking guy emerged from the bathroom stall and smirked. Locking eyes with Jack, the cocky guy washed his hands, dried them on a paper towel, and tucked the used, wet towel into Jack's white penguin shirt. The man tweaked Jack's plastic penguin beak and left.

The humiliating experience left a bitter taste in his mouth. Standing in a fast food restaurant bathroom, making minimum wage, dressed like a penguin was a far cry from the VP office he had worked hard for, deserved, and pridefully occupied.

"You can do this," he told his reflection. "You can do this for the kids. You can do this for Sheryl." Squaring his penguin shoulders, he grabbed the door handle.

Eddie spotted him as soon as he exited the bathroom. "There you are. Get over here, let's go."

The manager led him behind the counter to the register. A long line of grumpy customers clambered to give their orders. Eddie's rapid-fire spiel about the use of the register buttons instantly overwhelmed Jack.

His heart thudded as he looked into the impatient eyes of the first man in line.

"I'll take a Artie Burger with a large fry and give me a medium cheeser. No, make that a large."

Jack's hand trembled as he tried to enter the order.

"And a chocolate shake instead of a soda." The man changed his mind again to include both the shake and the soda while Jack continued to search the register for the Artie Burger button.

Eddie impatiently leaned over his shoulder and pointed. "Artie. Right there."

"Got it." Jack looked back to the customer. "Now, was that a meal or just the sandwich?"

The man stared angrily at Jack, and turned to Eddie. "Is he serious? I just told him."

Jack jumped in. "Yes, sir. I know. I'm new. I'm sorry. Could you please repeat the rest of your order?"

The man rolled his eyes and, faking sign language as he spoke, gave his order as though Jack was mentally impaired. "L-a-r-g-e f-r-y … c-h-o-c-o-l-a-t-e s-h-a-k-e, … l-a-r-g-e c-h-e-e-s-e-r…"

The next customer in line made an exaggerated movement to look at his watch, then leaned over the first customer's shoulder and grumbled at Jack. "How long is this going to take, buddy? Some of us have real jobs to get to."

Eddie called to the kitchen. "Large cheeser!"

Two young women working the registers next to Jack giggled. They seemed to be amused by Eddie's firm leadership. He winked at them, enjoying the opportunity to exercise his authority.

Jack flushed. "Right. Thank you. Will that be all?"

The customer threw up his hands in frustration. "I can't believe this guy. If I wanted more, I would have ordered it. Yes. That's all. Thank you. Take my money."

"Right. Okay, your total comes to $7.26."

The customer handed him a ten and turned to Eddie. "Make sure I get all my change."

Jack flinched at the shrill scream of a child who looked about three years old in the middle of the line that snaked back to the condiment counter. Her mother picked up the unhappy preschooler who continued to cry. Agitated by the noise, customers cast accusing glances to the mother and child, and then to the employees as if expecting the workers to quiet the situation. Feeling unnerved, Jack fought an urge to ditch his Arctic Artie's beak and head for home.

As the line moved closer by one more customer, Jack could hear the mother of the shrieking child calmly speak to her charge while perusing the menu. "Michelle, stop it. Mommy's trying to read."

Michelle. Hearing his daughter's name reminded him of why he stood in the chaos of this condescending establishment to provide service to these rude people. Jack was here for his family.

He could imagine catching Kimmy and swinging her into the air. Dropping into his big leather chair, Michelle would run up, giggling, and sit on the arm, hugging him. Sheryl would plop herself in his lap pushing Kimmy to the side and Adam would kneel down beside the chair. They would all laugh. Sheryl would look lovingly into his eyes. She would murmur, "I love you, Jack Baker."

"Double stack with fries," interrupted Jack's reverie. He saw the endless line and the snarling customers and smiled. His family was easily worth this stress. He took a deep breath and focused on the customer.

"And would you like a large drink on this wonderful day, sir?"

The startled customer responded, "Yeah, orange. An orange drink and switch those fries for onion rings."

"No, problem." Jack scanned the register for the right buttons. In a moment he located each item, noting that his lack of anxiety made the task easier. "Your total is a mere $6.17."

He counted back the customer's change and turned his attention to the next person in line. "And what may I have the chefs prepare for you, ma'am?"

The woman lifted her chin. "You're cheery."

"I have a lot to be cheery about." Jack stood taller in his penguin suit. "What can I get for you?"

As Jack suddenly took control of his job and began to work the crowd, he could see Eddie's expression. The manager's face seemed to say, "What just happened?" Jack almost wanted to laugh. Almost.

Two hours later, the noon rush began to ebb. Scattered customers remained in the dining area, lingering over cold fries. At his register, an exhausted Jack felt encouraged by what he had pulled off.

Eddie came up and patted him on the back. "I gotta hand it to you, old man. I've never seen anybody catch on as fast as you. Keep it up and you just might be back next week. Nice job."

Jack gave him a tired smile. "Thanks, Eddie. You mind if I call my wife really quick? I want to make sure the kids are okay."

Eddies eyebrows shot skyward. "Making calls on the clock? I thought that was just a chick thing." Eddie fisted him on the arm. "Aw, you earned it. Hang up the moment you see a customer."

As Jack pushed buttons on his cell phone, he could hear Eddie in the kitchen flirting with the girls. He put the phone to his ear, but instead of the familiar ring, he heard a series of clicks followed by a recorded message. "Your wireless service has been temporarily disconnected. To reconnect service, please press forty-four to be connected to a customer service representative. Message 132c."

Jack moaned. "You've got to be kidding me." He dropped the useless phone into his pocket.

The restaurant door opened and Jack looked up to attend to the next customer. Seeing his former assistant enter, Jack swallowed back pangs of humiliation. Wesley swaggered to the counter, and Jack noticed a surprised recognition cross his face, quickly followed by cunning calculation. Inwardly, Jack cringed. Outwardly, he stood with his penguin chest puffed out.

Wesley grinned. He seemed to be savoring sweet revenge. "Jack Baker?" Overly loud, he called out in a hearty tone of voice. "Is that you in that spiffy penguin get-up?" He came close and inspected Jack's costume. "Nice duds, man, definitely a change from the designer threads you wore at the office."

Jack grasped the irony. He recalled the day he had introduced Wesley to Mr. Fergusson as his assistant. Now he would fill Wesley's lunch order. "Hi, Wesley. How have you been?"

"Better than you, I see. Wow, so this is the next step. Not quite what I had envisioned, but hey, you've gotta follow your dreams, right?"

"You gotta put food on the table, Wesley. What can I get for you?"

Wesley's booming voice was laced with sarcasm. "Oh, that's so sad. Mr. Big-time Executive has to crawl around with the lowly in order to feed the family. Oops—I think I feel a tear." He wiped at his cheek.

Jack puzzled over Wesley's attitude. He had given the guy a job, believed in him, and defended him to the boss. Now this. He didn't get it. "Have your fun," he said softly.

Wesley swiped under his eye again. "Yep, there's moisture. But wait … no, it's a tear of joy because I finally get to tell you what to do. Bummer. For a moment I thought I was experiencing the warm, fuzzy feelings caring people often speak of. Oh well, at least I've found my new hotspot for lunch. Give me an Artie Burger, a large soda, a small fry—watching my figure—and, let's see … a triple order of giddy joy. I'm willing to pay for it. But then, it looks like that one's on you, doesn't it?"

Without comment, Jack rang up Wesley's order. "$5.86."

"Oh, I can't wait to tell everyone at the office. I'm so excited, I think I'm going to burst."

Wesley retrieved his wallet, making a show of fanning the bills before selecting a $20. He handed the bill to Jack but held tight to it for a second before he released the money. His smile was euphoric.

Jack looked him in the eye, trying to keep any expression from his face. "Your order is number 212. Thanks."

"No," responded Wesley with oily exaggeration. "Thank you."

Chapter Twenty-four

George Fergusson was intent on a column of figures that were not making him happy when he was interrupted by a knock on the doorframe. He looked up to see a beaming Wesley. He felt exasperated just looking at the guy. He took off his glasses and rubbed his eyes. "What do you want?"

Wesley strode into the office. "I just thought you might like to know where I went for lunch today. I'm telling everyone."

Fergusson raised an eyebrow. "Why would I care where you ate lunch?"

Uninvited, Wesley pulled up a chair and sat down. Fergusson frowned. "Because I went to Arctic Artie's where I was served by our dear friend, Jack Baker."

Fergusson felt a sudden tightness in his chest. This could be bad. "He's working at Arctic Artie's?"

Wesley beamed with the news.

Fergusson analyzed the situation before speaking almost to himself. "He's more desperate than I thought. He's never been willing to relocate before, but if he gets an offer from Puriease now, he just might take it." He came around the desk and towered over his seated subordinate. "This is bad. We need to remind him of why he wants to stay in Wooded Falls." He pointed to Wesley. "And you're going to be the one to do it."

He cringed at Wesley's gleeful giggle.

Wesley clapped his hands. "Ooh, a diabolical plan. How exciting."

Chapter Twenty-five

Sheryl was standing at the kitchen counter fixing supper when she heard the door from the garage close. Jack entered the living room, tossed his jacket on the chair, and stretched out on the sofa. She turned off the stove and hurried to the living room.

"How was my working man's first day on the job?" She leaned over the back of the sofa and kissed him on the cheek.

He stared at the blank TV screen. "I don't know how these kids do it. It's hard work and everybody treats you like a bum who should be honored to get them a two-dollar burger. What happened to common respect?"

"Not so common anymore."

The phone rang, but Sheryl made no move to answer.

"You going to get that?" Jack rested his arm over his eyes.

"Nope. It's probably just another collection agency. They've been calling every few hours and I still don't have money to pay them. I figure if I don't answer, they'll give up after a day or two."

Jack turned toward her. "Did you know our cell phones were shut off?"

She nodded. "We'll get them turned back on when you get paid."

Jack's face took on his lost puppy expression. "I feel like part of me is missing without my cell phone. Like I'm disconnected from society. I wish they would've given us some warning before they shut them off."

Oops. So much for trying to protect him. She came around the end of the sofa and sat down next to him. "They did warn us, sweetie. We got a letter several weeks ago. I found the notice in the stack of unopened bills. You kind of have to keep opening the mail, even though we don't have any money, just to stay aware of what's happening with things."

Jack sighed. "I know. I've let things get out of hand."

"But enough of that. Tell me more about your day."

Jack shook his head. "It's not that interesting. I'm just looking forward to that first check."

"Me too." Sheryl brightened. "We need to do some Christmas shopping, but I'd like to get the kids new winter coats first."

"First we catch up on the bills. Mortgage and cell phones."

"Yeah, it will be nice to get back to normal."

But two weeks later, Jack and Sheryl stared at the paycheck in silent disbelief.

"Can that be right?" Sheryl searched for an additional zero or two at the end of the number.

"I asked Eddie, and he said the amount is correct."

She reread the miniscule amount. "For the whole two weeks?"

"Yep."

"We can't even make a mortgage payment with this."

"Nope."

Sheryl felt a dark wave of discouragement wash over her. "Are you sure you don't want me to look for work?"

"Absolutely not. We've discussed that enough. You need to be at home with the kids."

"Then you need another job."

"Yep."

The ring of the phone sent a shock up her spine. Neither moved to answer it and the answering machine clicked on. "You've reached the Bakers. Please leave a message."

An automated voice left a message as one machine talked to another. "This is the law office of Baxter, Brown, Boxwielder, and Dunn. We need to speak with you immediately in regards to your delinquent Banner Card account. Please return this call as soon as possible."

"Well," Sheryl reasoned, "it's not enough to pay any bills. Wanna go grocery shopping?"

Chapter Twenty-six

Kim squealed with joy as Jack swung her high into the air and settled her into the shopping cart. He pushed the cart down the first aisle of the grocery superstore and felt gleeful as he led his family on their first shopping spree in a long time. Who cared that they were merely purchasing groceries.

Sheryl quickly filled the cart with colorful produce and Jack added a gourmet cheese spread. By the time the Bakers were three quarters through the store, the cart was half full.

Adam waved a package of chocolate chip cookies. "Mom, can we get these?"

"Sure," Sheryl quickly replied.

Adam beamed as he put them in the cart. Michelle reached for a box of cereal from a center display. "Can we get these?"

"Why not?" Sheryl smiled at the enthusiasm of her children.

In the freezer section, Kim pointed to the row of ice cream. She looked at Jack with round, begging eyes. "Do can get these?"

"Yes, we 'do can get' those." Jack selected a container and added the store brand chocolate to the cart. He felt deep satisfaction at his family finding happiness in being together on this simple shopping trip.

Steering the cart into the meat market, he selected a large turkey. As he pushed the turkey into the rack under the cart, Jack said, "Can't host the annual Bible study group Thanksgiving dinner without this bad boy."

Sheryl tucked a gallon of milk and a carton of eggs in the available spaces in the cart. "This feels good. I feel like 'us' again. Nothing could ruin this moment."

At the checkout, Adam and Michelle transferred groceries onto the conveyer belt as the young cashier ran the items through the scanner. Jack felt a sudden tightness in his chest as the total rapidly surpassed their cash on hand. Panicked, he looked at Sheryl. He could tell by her sudden paleness that she too realized what had happened.

The cashier finished their order with a flourish. "Your total comes to $127.49."

"Ah, you know what?" Jack leaned close to the cashier whose nametag read Stuart. "I'm not sure we need all of this, Stuart." He pulled several items from the bags. "This can go. And this isn't really necessary." He handed the items to the cashier who pressed some keys on the register to delete the amounts.

"Oh, this isn't working. The computer doesn't like me." Now the cashier looked genuinely nervous. "Computers never like me. Mr. Henry's going to kill me. This is the third time I've paged him since lunch."

Noting the long line of waiting customers, the cashier turned on a flashing assistance-needed sign. Several customers groaned. Jack's public humiliation grew with each flash of the light.

Jack tried to defuse the situation by making casual conversation. "Tough boss?"

The young man pulled out a piece of paper and nervously scribbled a few words. His voice sounded friendly and positive as he said, "No, not at all. He's a beautiful human who cares for small animals and sends toy drums and lollipops to orphans in Norwegian villages."

He slid the note to Jack who read the hastily printed words: "Can't talk. The cash registers are bugged. Tell my mom I love her."

Jack wasn't sure if he should laugh or take Stuart seriously. "Can we cancel the order and start over?"

Stuart shook his head. "Can't. Mr. Henry has to do it. We need his key, which I don't have 'cause I'm not a manager and only managers are allowed to have a key, so I don't."

A short balding man with a gold nametag approached the line as though the Bakers had been busted for shoplifting. He gave Jack a quick once over, then turned to the young cashier.

"What's the problem, Stewie?" His nasally voice made Jack's tense nerves tighter.

"Um, these guys need to take some of these things off their order so I need your password again. I'm sorry."

The manager whirled around to the Bakers. "Is there a problem with these items?"

"No, no, they're fine." Jack didn't think this should be such a big deal. "We just decided that we don't need them."

"Then why did you put them in your cart?" He spoke to Jack as if addressing a simpleton. Jack looked at Sheryl, whose face had turned red with embarrassment. People in line behind them were taking an interest in their situation.

Jack wasn't certain why he needed to explain their decision. "We thought we needed them at first and then realized we don't."

The manager shielded the computer with his body as he entered his top-secret password and then turned back to Jack. "You thought you needed them. I see. Well, let me make a quick phone call here …"

Snap! Using his cell phone, the manager took a picture of Jack.

"I've got your mug, now! I'm going to put this in my file. You see those cameras?" The manager pointed at the security cameras hanging from the ceiling. "Those are my eyes in the sky. Next time you come in this store, I'll be watching you, and if you try any funny business, I will take you down. You hearing me? Shoplifters aren't prosecuted here. They disappear."

Jack again fought conflicting emotions. Should he be amused or angry? "I see. Is this standard store procedure for returning items?"

The manager pointed at his nameplate. "Look at this. What do you think that says?"

"It says store manager."

"Seventeen years of duty, son. I've seen it all, and I drop the hammer hard. Store manager. That means Commander-in-Chief. Judge, jury, and jailer. That title on this little beauty means that whatever I do is store procedure."

Sheryl turned away from the manager, keeping her attention focused on the children. Michelle and Adam pressed closer to their parents. Sheryl lifted Kim from the shopping cart and held her tightly.

Customers behind them murmured amongst themselves at this obvious circus scene. "I saw him on the news," Jack heard one woman say to another customer.

"Oh, my, yes," replied another. "Is he in trouble again?"

With hurt showing in her eyes, Sheryl steered the children out of the checkout line to wait ahead of Jack. At least there they would be out of earshot from the drama unfolding between the overly paranoid manager and the gossiping customers waiting to purchase their own groceries.

Stuart finished running the new numbers for the Bakers. "Um, your new total is $87.14."

Jack handed over the bills. "Here's ninety. Keep the change." He looked at the manager who stood with arms folded, and a sneer on his face, watching. As they pushed their cart past him, Jack said, "Sorry for the inconvenience."

Catching up with Sheryl and the children, he noticed she was paying particular attention to the shopper at the adjacent checkout counter. In the next lane, a woman handed a card to the cashier.

The clerk deftly swiped the card and pointed to an item, "The food stamp card can't be used for this, so your cash total is $1.15."

The customer handed the money to the clerk. Without any of the hassle they had experienced, the other shopper exited the store alongside of the Bakers with a cart full of bagged groceries.

Chapter Twenty-seven

November 24, 2011

Sheryl mentally ran down her to-do list as she surveyed the holiday table. Smells of sliced roast turkey stacked on the holiday serving tray mingled with the piquant pumpkin pies cooling on the sideboard. Steaming gravy boats set at each end of the table next to baskets of whole-wheat rolls and relish trays of tart green olives, dill pickle spears, and festive pickled beets.

The doorbell rang and voices from the living room told her that their last expected guest had arrived. And just in time.

"Is there anything I can do to help?" Marissa came into the kitchen of the Baker home, removed the covering from her sweet potato casserole, and set the dish on the laden table.

"You can light the candles." Sheryl handed her friend a lighter. "I'll set out the veggies and our Thanksgiving Day feast will be ready."

From the family room came the sound of friendly camaraderie and laughter. The Bible study group had been meeting for several years and this was their third Thanksgiving dinner together.

Sheryl scanned the table one more time. The food was plentiful and the table with all of the extra leaves looked elegant with plenty of room for the four couples and three of the littlest children. The older children had their own table in the family room. The families would gather together for Thanksgiving prayer and then separate to their tables.

Sheryl caught Jack's attention. "Call the kids. We're ready."

In moments, the adults moved to the dining room and settled the little ones into the high chairs and booster seats. Chairs scraped and were pulled to the table as everyone found their places and the children gathered beside their parents. Kim reached into a dish and popped an olive into her mouth, resembling a squirrel with a nut in her cheek.

Sheryl turned to Jack. "Sweetie, would you bless the meal?"

Looking once again like the confident leader of their home, Jack paused until everyone was quiet and expectant. Closing his eyes, he took a deep breath. "Dear Lord—"

The phone rang. Icy fear jolted through her veins and Sheryl looked at Jack. Would a collection agency call on Thanksgiving Day? What if a message went to the answering machine and their friends heard?

Jack must have had the same thoughts. He sounded urgent when he said, "Honey, why don't you see who that is?"

"Ah, let the machine get it. Let's eat," said Marissa's husband, Bill.

The phone rang again. How many rings until the machine kicked in? Panicked, Sheryl started toward the phone.

"It's Thanksgiving. We need to be thankful for everything—even friends who call at dinnertime," stammered Jack.

"I'll tell them I'll call back," said Sheryl at the same time.

Her guests were silent, watching, as Sheryl picked up the receiver. The interruption had come at the most inopportune moment just as dishes piled with cornbread stuffing, creamy mashed potatoes, and rosy cranberry sauce should be noisily, joyfully passed from one to another.

She turned an apologetic smile to the family and friends seated around the table as she spoke into the phone. "Hello? Oh, hi, it's so good to hear from you." A stern voice on the other end reminded her that they were overdue … she didn't wait to hear anymore. "We've got to catch up, but you know what? We're sitting down to dinner." The nasally response was louder, more demanding. Sheryl cheerily cut in again, hoping she didn't sound as fake as she felt. "Can I call you back? Great. We'll talk then. Bye-bye."

Sheryl returned to her chair and breathed a sigh of relief as all heads bowed to give thanks.

Jack began to pray. "Most gracious Heavenly Father, we thank you for this bountiful meal—"

The telephone noisily interrupted again. Sheryl's heart thudded.

"Whoops!" Jack looked up. "Honey, you want to get that?"

Bill drummed his fingers and sounded impatient. "Come on, Jack. Just finish the blessing."

Sheryl nervously started toward the phone. "I'll get it. You go ahead without me."

She grabbed the phone and carried the offending interruption into the hallway behind the kitchen. She heard Jack continue with his prayer. "Uh … we're grateful for all of the wonderful things you have provided. Please bless this meal. In Jesus's name, amen."

Sheryl spoke over the spiel of the collection agency representative and practically spat the words. "This is Thanksgiving Day. Do not call us today." She hit the off button and stared at the phone in anger.

She heard the clang of silverware on china and laughter as people took helpings of traditional Thanksgiving dishes and passed them around the table. With piled plates, the older children rushed down the steps to the family room. She heard Bill say, "All right, this is what it's all about."

Sheryl returned to the table and leaned toward Jack. "I turned off the phone so we can enjoy our guests."

Jack looked relieved. "Fantastic idea."

The food and the fellowship were enjoyable, yet Sheryl felt phony and on edge since they had not chosen to tell even their closest friends about their financial situation. But Jack had been insistent that they would soon be through this temporary bad patch and there was no sense burdening their friends with their misery.

When they finished the after-dessert coffee, the ladies helped Sheryl clear the table. Bill turned to Fred, "Hey, what time does the game start?"

Fred checked his watch. "Eight minutes ago."

All of the men simultaneously rushed to the living room.

Fred called over his shoulder, "Wonderful meal, Sheryl, as usual."

The men settled in chairs and Jack pressed the button on the remote. The television came on but the screen remained black except for a floating "searching for signal" notice. Collecting the nearly empty tray of turkey meat from the dining table, Sheryl observed Jack's eyebrows come together in confusion. He pointed the remote and pushed several buttons. Nothing.

"What's wrong?" Fred glanced over Jack's shoulder.

Ron chimed in, "What's up with your TV, Baker? The game is in play."

"I'm not sure." Jack sounded puzzled.

Bill moaned. "Your cable isn't out, is it?"

Sheryl saw panic on Jack's face. Of course! We haven't paid the bill.

"It worked earlier today," he responded. "The kids watched the parade up here."

"Let me have a look at her!" Fred pulled out the TV and checked the cables. "Everything looks good back here."

The other wives had paused their cleanup operation and were watching the crisis in progress. Suddenly, the answering machine clicked on. Sheryl's recorded voice sounded perky. "You've reached the Bakers. Please leave a message."

Jack looked at Sheryl in shock. "Didn't you turn that off?"

"I thought I did," she choked out. Panicked, she hurried around the counter to the phone. She picked up the receiver and nervously punched at buttons to stop the answering machine but the automated message clearly announced, "This is the law office of Baxter, Brown, Boxwielder, and Dunn. We need to speak with you immediately in regards to your delinquent Banner Card account. Please return this call."

At the end of the message beep, the eyes of all four couples looked at one another in confused silence. End of message. End of masquerade.

"Oops," said Sheryl weakly. "I guess I turned off the ringer."

Marissa broke the awkward silence. "Must be a mistake." She patted Sheryl's arm. "Don't worry about it."

"Back to the game." Fred turned his attention to the TV, but as he looked from the blank screen to Jack, a certain understanding dawned. He cleared his throat. "Perhaps we should be going."

Fred sounded tentative, but the others nodded in relief. Bill called for the children to come, and Fred went to the bedroom to get coats. Marissa scooped her dishes into her picnic basket. While their longtime friends collected belongings and children, Jack came to stand by his wife. Sheryl felt vulnerable and about to be abandoned.

As the guests reached the front door, Fred called out, "We can watch the game at my place. I've got the surround sound all hooked up and ready to go." He leaned around Ron and called to Jack, "You coming?"

Jack flushed. "No, I'll stick around and help clean up. Let me know who wins."

Marissa gave Sheryl a quick hug and then their friends were gone.

"They couldn't have gotten out faster if the house was on fire." Sheryl choked back tears.

Jack closed the front door and turned to his family. The children looked at their parents with questioning eyes. "Why don't you kids go up to your rooms for a while? I'll come up later."

Adam moved close to Sheryl. "Mom, are you okay?"

Jack patted him on the back. "She's fine, kiddo, go on up. I'll be there soon."

The children trudged their way upstairs. Jack wrapped his arms around Sheryl and held her. Like a long restrained avalanche that finally tore loose, shaking, silent sobs poured forth.

"Hey, sweetie." He pressed her head to his shoulder.

Suddenly she pushed away, her arms pressed to her sides and her hands clenched into tight fists. "Why couldn't you keep your job? None of this would be happening if you could have kept your job!"

"That wasn't my call, Sheryl." He reached for her.

But she didn't want him to touch her. To hold her. She wanted to be mad. To be mad at him. She backed away. "Well, why didn't you include more safety warnings in your marketing? You should have gotten approval before you ran out and had labels printed. You always think you're right. Why are you so bull-headed?"

He gently approached and took her hand. She held herself stiffly.

"Sweetie, we're going through a hard time right now and life is a little embarrassing but we can't turn on each other. We're all we've got." He stroked her hair. "The only way we're going to make it is if we stay together—physically and emotionally."

She sighed and let him pull her close. Her face against her shirt, she wept great heaving sobs. She heard his voice soft in her ear but couldn't make out the words. Finally spent, she pulled away from his soggy, wet shoulder and met his eyes.

"I'm sorry. I love you. I love you so much." And she meant it. The anger was gone, spilled out and flushed away.

"We're going to get through this," he promised.

Sheryl hesitated and then looked away. "I want to apply for food stamps."

Jack stared at his wife in shock. "What?"

Sheryl continued with more energy, rubbing her arms as she spoke. "I mean, we've been paying for other people to use them for twenty years, right? They exist for people in our situation who need help in a bind. That's what they're for." She waited for his answer, her eyes pleading for him to understand.

Jack paced the hallway rubbing his neck. "Sweetie … Sweetie." He shook his head.

"Your Arctic Artie checks barely cover gas to get you to work. We'll need groceries again soon, Jack." Sheryl motioned toward the stairs where the children had gone to their rooms. "I'm not going to let my pride starve the kids. I won't do it. I have no pride left to protect. We need to survive now."

Chapter Twenty-eight

November 29, 2011

The Tuesday following their embarrassing Thanksgiving dinner with the Bible study group, Sheryl woke up determined. Ever since the shakedown at the grocery store when the store manager had harassed them for returning items, Sheryl had not been able to get the picture of the other shopper, the woman with the food stamps, out of her mind.

With Adam and Michelle off to school, and Jack at Arctic Artie's, Sheryl bundled Kim in her coat and buckled the little girl into her car seat. Driving downtown and mumbling to herself, Sheryl compared the addresses on the city buildings against the numbers she had copied from the phone book onto a piece of scratch paper.

Finally, she had a match. "Bingo," she announced to Kim who was listening to the Christmas carols playing over the radio, her eyes heavy. Sheryl turned and parked in front of the government office.

She turned off the motor, but instead of opening the door, she dropped her hands into her lap and absently fingered the keys. She sat like that for a long time, watching through her windshield as a few people came and went from the office.

When the window began to fog and she felt herself shiver, Sheryl sent up a quiet prayer. "Please, God, don't let anyone see me."

Careful not to wake the sleeping Kim, she pulled her from the car seat and rested the child against her shoulder. Walking toward the building, she glanced nervously around, hoping to avoid being noticed. Crossing her path, an old man looked from her to her destination. Meeting his glance, Sheryl offered a friendly smile but he narrowed his eyes as he studied her up and down.

"You're not starving," he accused.

The ferocity of the stranger's judgment took the air from her lungs, and Sheryl stopped to catch her breath. She stared after him, but he never looked back as he made his way to his car in the parking lot.

Feeling doubly humiliated, Sheryl turned to go back to her car. But when Kim stirred in her arms, Sheryl remembered she had come to this place for her children. She would swallow a lot of pride to feed her precious babies. Tightening her hold on Kim, Sheryl turned once more and walked directly into the food stamp office.

The office was stuffy. Though there were several visitors in addition to a staff worker manning the counter and more staff working in cubicles behind the counter, the atmosphere was quiet and awkward.

A woman with over-permed hair met Sheryl at the counter. "Can I help you?"

"I'm here to get food stamps," Sheryl said softly.

Cupping a hand behind an ear, the woman spoke louder. "What was that?"

Sheryl leaned closer. "Food stamps," she repeated. "I'm here—"

The woman handed her a clipboard with a stack of paperwork and a pen. "Have a seat and fill those out. Someone will call you."

"I see," Sheryl murmured as she juggled the still sleeping Kim and the clipboard.

At the row of uncomfortable plastic chairs, Sheryl carefully laid Kim down so her head was in Sheryl's lap. Balancing the clipboard off to her other side, she began filling out the endless blank lines. The people that ran the program wanted to know a lot of things that seemed to her to be none of their business. But, she shrugged, they were the ones who had the money and she was asking that they give some to her.

When Kim yawned and stirred, Sheryl checked her watch. She had been here already for an hour. Her back ached from holding her youngest while filling in the paperwork in the unfriendly chair. At least Kim had gotten a good nap.

"Mommy?"

Sheryl gathered Kim onto her lap. "Shhhhh. It's okay, honey."

"Mrs. Baker," called the permed woman.

Sheryl nudged Kim's feet to the floor, took her hand, and the two of them followed the clerk. The woman stood aside and indicated they should go into the next cubicle.

Stepping inside, Sheryl observed a woman at her desk, her head bent over the forms Sheryl had filled out earlier. The air was stuffier here than in the waiting room. Self-conscious, Sheryl shifted her weight, squeezing Kim's hand until she squirmed in her grasp.

"Sorry," Sheryl whispered to her daughter.

The woman looked up and waved them to a chair. "Have a seat."

Sheryl sat, lifting Kim into the chair next to her.

"So you have three kids?" Older than Sheryl, the woman's tone seemed lifeless. "One adopted?" She looked pointedly over her spectacles at Kim.

Sheryl nodded. "Yes, that's right."

"And two vehicles."

Sheryl nodded again. "Yes."

"Any savings, stocks, bonds?"

Sheryl shook her head. "We've pretty much cashed in everything to put food on the table. We even had to sell our stock, but I guess you should know that, being that you ended up with most of the money in taxes, huh?" Sheryl felt her weak smile dim at her poor attempt at humor.

"Mmm, hmmm. Trust me, no extra money skipped into my paycheck." Robotically, the woman, whose nametag had Janice printed in perfect black letters, continued to scan the paperwork. "Well, it looks like I'll be able to authorize $625 per month."

Sheryl leaned forward eagerly. "Are you serious?"

"It's prorated, so you're only going to get about $100 for the rest of November, but your December deposit will post on the fifth. You should receive a card in the mail in the next two weeks or so."

"Thank you." Relief made Sheryl feel giddy. She grabbed up Kim and hugged her. "Thank you so much. I can't even tell you how wonderful this is." Still burbling, Sheryl stood and pumped the woman's hand vigorously. "This is a temporary situation, believe me, but thank you so much for helping us get through it. You have a very Merry Christmas!"

"You, too, dear," Janice returned flatly, extricating her hand from Sheryl's and flexing her fingers.

Sheryl swung Kim into her arms and, with visions of Christmas ham and all the trimmings dancing through her head, nearly skipped from the office.

Chapter Twenty-nine

Jack tapped the order into the register and scanned the room while his customer decided between large and supersized. Only a few tables were occupied. Only one person left in line. The afternoon calm had arrived.

"Supersize," was the final answer.

"All right, that comes to $7.14. Your order number is 322. Thank you." Jack handed the customer his change and looked up as the door opened. As his former assistant sauntered in with a smirk on his face, Jack groaned inwardly. Today must be make-fun-of-Jack time again. "Hello, Wesley. What can I get for you?"

"Hey, Jack." He paused and transformed his expression. "I want to apologize for the last time I was in here."

Was that sincerity in Wesley's voice? Jack shifted his weight and studied this turn of attitude.

Wesley looked contrite. "I acted like an inconsiderate snob."

That was true.

"And that's just not me."

That certainly wasn't true.

Jack opened his mouth but couldn't think of anything to say.

Wesley continued, "Well, okay, it's very much me. It's my calling card, but for some reason, I felt this strange, almost guilt-like emotion after smothering your few remaining shreds of self-esteem, so I want to apologize."

Jack thought of the hopes he had for this young man. Maybe he wasn't completely incorrigible. "No need to apologize, but thank you. All is forgiven."

Wesley folded his arms and stared at the menu on the back wall. "Well, I did a little more than that. I told Fergusson that you were working here."

Jack's shoulders slumped at this revelation. He had seen Mr. Fergusson as a father figure and wanted to please him. He didn't want Mr. Fergusson to know where he worked now. "Why would you do that?"

Wesley held up his hands defensively. "I didn't say that the remorse was immediate. The previously foreign feeling developed shortly after smearing your name around the office. At any rate, Fergie didn't see the humor quite as I had planned. In fact, he said he's considering giving you your job back."

Jack felt a jolt of astonishment. And something else he hadn't experienced in a long time. Hope? "When?"

Wesley shook his head. "It's not a done deal but looks promising. Your name is kind of the kiss of death right now but he's going to make a few calls and try to clear things up. He said the Good for Us line is your baby and he needs you to run it."

Jack leaned over the counter toward Wesley. "This isn't funny, Wesley. Don't expect to share giggles if you've got some kind of punch line coming."

Reaching for a napkin, Wesley swiped the counter between them. Crumbs and moisture from overfull drink cups dropped off the edge onto Jack's feet. "No punch line, Jack. This comes directly from Fergs. Now, there may be a few months before he can get you back in, but he did say that he might be able to cut you a Christmas bonus as a measure of good faith." He wadded the dirty napkin and aimed for the trash behind the counter. The paper ball hit the rim and fell to the floor.

Jack rubbed his forehead, disbelief and optimism warring in his mind. His nightmare might be coming to an end. He might be waking up to a beautiful future. He decided he would dare to hope. He smiled at Wesley. "You are making my day. Right now you are making my month."

Wesley looked away. "Yeah, that puts a warm, cozy little fire right smack in the middle of my soul, but don't get all gushy on me. I was thinking that perhaps, since I basically rekindled all of this, a promotion may be in order. I'm not really the assistant type."

Jack laughed aloud. "Wesley, if you get me my job back, I will make you my consultant, my partner. You can be my direct supervisor for all I care."

Wesley stared into space as if carefully examining the situation. "Okay, okay, partner would be special. I don't think the Fergmeister would go for direct supervisor but I'm game for dreaming. I wonder what it would sound like to hear you call me 'sir.'"

Jack's brain spun to a stop. Wesley had a disarming way of keeping him off balance. After an awkward pause, Wesley cleared his throat and cocked his head to the side, as if to say, "I'm waiting, Jack. Get on with it."

Jack's voice sounded tentative when he finally spoke. "I … I bet it would sound very natural … sir."

Placing his hand across his heart, Wesley smiled as if in bliss. "Here. Right here. I feel tingles." He closed his eyes. "Tingles." His eyes popped open and he reached across the counter to slap Jack on the arm. "Why don't we stick with that for now? It'll be good to have you back, Baker."

Wesley was halfway to the door when Jack called to him, "Thank you, Wesley. And say thanks to Mr. Fergusson for me."

Wesley held his hand to his ear without turning back, as though listening for something.

Jack said the word for the second time. "Sir."

Chapter Thirty

Michelle put the final leg on Mr. Potato Head when her mom burst into the living room singing at the top of her lungs. Her overly dramatic opera style assured the world that life was good. On the sofa, Kim, Michelle, and Michelle's friend, eight-year-old Barbara Ann, gazed at her in wonder.

Keeping her eyes on Sheryl as she waltzed through the room, Barbara Ann whispered, "What's up with your mom?"

Sheryl sang directly to the girls and danced around the couch and out of the room. Michelle was bewildered.

"What's up with your mom?" asked Barbara Ann again.

"I don't know." Michelle leaned forward to watch her mother dance into the kitchen. "That's the happiest I've seen her since Dad lost his job."

Barbara Ann looked horrified as she turned to Michelle. "Your dad lost his job?"

Michelle nodded. "Months ago. Now our TV doesn't work, and our phone rings all the time but we're not allowed to answer it."

Barbara Ann frowned. "How do you pay for stuff without money?"

Michelle shrugged. "I don't know."

"What if he doesn't have a job before Christmas?" Barbara Ann lowered her voice. "Will you guys still get presents?"

Michelle thought for a moment. "I don't know."

Kim scrambled off the couch to stand in front of them. She put one hand on each girl's arm. "Presents?"

Michelle hadn't worried about Christmas or gifts before, but for Kim's sake, the holiday and traditions were important. She glanced at Barbara Ann and saw concern reflected in her friend's face.

Barbara Ann's face brightened. "I have an idea."

Moments later, the girls were hauling items from Michelle's room to a table set up outside on the driveway. The commotion brought Adam from his room where he had been doing homework. "What's the big project?"

"We're selling stuff," Michelle informed. "To help Mom and Dad."

"A garage sale." Barbara Ann shifted a pair of ice skates Michelle had outgrown into her other hand. "Got anything to sell?"

Adam considered for a moment and nodded.

"Bring it outside," Michelle instructed.

Chapter Thirty-one

That evening, Jack arrived home to find several cars parked near his house and people milling around his driveway. He parked down the street, relieved that none of the cars were from news stations. At the bottom of the driveway, Kim sat at her small table presiding over a collection of paper cups. In Michelle's handwriting, a sign next to Kim's piggybank read, "Lemonade—twenty-five cents."

Spotting her dad, Kim grinned and handed him a half-full cup. Jack took the cup and lifted Kim into his arms. She wrapped her arms around his neck, her hands sticky from lemonade.

"What's all this?" Jack squelched back embarrassment as strangers looked over items from his household.

Michelle's face beamed with enthusiasm. "Barbara Ann and I are having a garage sale. And we're making money."

A mother with a toddler in tow handed money to Michelle. "Here you go, honey. These V-Slams were all sold out last Christmas. My kids will be so excited when I bring this home."

Jack recalled scoring the last game at the big box store last year. Now his hard-won prize was going home with a stranger for a quarter of the original price. He glanced at Adam, who was showing a young boy how to use the Safari Vacation Kit. "Michelle," he began. But he couldn't extinguish the look of enthusiasm she turned to him. He knew the rush of marketing success, and she, along with Barbara Ann, Kim, and Adam were seeing the fruits of their creative efforts.

Jack smiled. After all, today was a good day, he had good news, and he wasn't going to squash the joy the kids were experiencing.

"Michelle," he began again. "I'm going inside to find your mom."

"Leave Kim with us," Barbara Ann instructed. "Everyone buys lemonade from her."

Jack had to admire the cuteness factor Kim brought to the table. Sticky fingers and all. He set his youngest back in her seat. He chugged his cup and exaggeratedly smacked his lips. "How about some for your mom?"

Delighted with her father's approval, Kim offered a second cup with a smile so big her eyes turned into half-moons.

In the house, Jack took in the table set with Sheryl's best china cups and a tall candle. The aroma of fresh brewed coffee was a welcome shift from his clothes that smelled of french fries. Beaming, he kissed his wife on the cheek and offered her Kim's lemonade.

"Kim has been selling this stuff as fast as I can stir it up from the powered mix." Sheryl set the cup on the counter. "Don't tell but I can't drink another swallow."

Jack hooked a thumb over his shoulder. "I can't say that I'm comfortable with what's going on out there."

Sheryl nodded. "I know. We agreed to keep our adult problems to ourselves, but they are smart kids. They noticed that no one got new school clothes this year, we are not answering the phone, and our meals are whatever creative mash-ups I can assemble from what we have in the pantry and what I can buy for nearly free." She handed him the lemonade. "Besides, they want to help. And isn't turning stuff into cash what marketing is all about?"

Jack conceded with a smile. "They are pretty good at sales. And intuitive enough to know with Kim's smile, they can sell lemonade in November." Noticing the table, his eyebrows raised in question. "Surprises inside and out. What's going on here?"

"Well," she looped her arms around his neck. "I had the most amazing day."

He nodded enthusiastically. "Me, too."

"And I have good news."

"I bet my good news is better than your good news," he taunted.

She stepped back, folded her arms, and eyed him coyly. "I accept your challenge."

"Ladies first." He gave a slight bow. "What have you got?"

"Well, I just happen to know a certain someone who went down to the food stamp office today, filled out an application, and was approved on the spot for $625 a month in groceries." She squealed with glee and hugged his neck.

"$625 a month?" He tried to remember the last time his wife had been so happy. "That's huge."

"Top that one, Mr. Baker."

"Well, let's see—where to begin?" He turned away and paused for dramatic effect. "For starters, I may not be working at Arctic Artie's much longer."

"Okay ..."

"Because—are you ready?" He swung around to face her. "You're standing. You should be sitting."

She playfully slapped him on the chest as he pointed her to a chair. "Would you tell me already."

He spoke slowly. "Well, I hear a well-known local manufacturer of cleaning supplies is launching a new, environmentally friendly line, and they need its innovator to spearhead the marketing."

Sheryl gasped. "You got your job back?"

Jack laughed. "You look surprised. Honestly, I can't believe Smythe-Andersson made it this long without me."

Sheryl cupped his face. "The nightmare is over."

"Wait," he continued. "It gets better."

"What? Tell me."

He paused, waiting for her to guess.

"Not the bonus," she whispered in wonder.

Jack grinned. "It's going to be a very Merry Christmas, baby!" He pulled her into his arms and whirled her around the kitchen. Barely keeping their balance, they laughed. What a wonder, he thought. How many days, weeks, months had gone by since the two of them had laughed? Really laughed? The welcome sound was joyful to his ears and good medicine to his weary heart.

Suddenly, Sheryl stopped the merriment. "We need to celebrate. We're going out to dinner. I am going to take you wherever you want to eat tonight."

"What? How? We don't have any money yet."

"I've got some emergency dollars tucked away."

Jack's feigned an exaggerated sense of horror. "Emergency money? I've been eating sticks, twigs, and dirt for three months. What have you been waiting for, a monsoon?"

She touched his nose with the tip of her finger. "There's not that much, but enough to celebrate the end of this nightmare. Let's tell the kids to get cleaned up."

They went to the garage and said hello to Barbara Ann's mother who had come by to pick up her daughter. With cups of lemonade in hand, mother and daughter waved as they drove away.

Kim shook her piggybank so Jack could hear the coins inside. Adam elbowed Michelle. "Not a bad idea. A lot of kids were pretty happy with their new loot."

Jack watched one shopper leave as another car pulled up. "Kids, when you are ready to close up your business for the evening, get in the van. We're going out for supper."

Chapter Thirty-two

That evening, a jubilant Baker family followed the hostess to their usual booth in their favorite Italian restaurant. Tiny Christmas sparkle lights had been added to the Tuscany décor and brilliant poinsettia blooms sat as centerpieces on each table.

Having enjoyed plenty of family nights in this very booth, they barely needed to look at the menu. After taking their order, the waitress disappeared, promising to be back in moments with drinks.

"Dad," Adam began, "we've been talking about you being employmentally challenged and all."

Jack winked at Sheryl. "Serious stuff." He turned to his children. "Shouldn't you be talking about more important things like video games and dolls?"

"I never talk about dolls," Adam assured.

"The doll part wasn't about you," Jack said and nodded toward the girls. "Go on, son."

"Well," Adam continued, "we were just wondering if Christmas is going to take one to the back of the knees this year."

Jack slipped an arm across the back of his wife's chair. "Are you asking if Santa is going to skip over our house because Daddy's making minimum wage?"

"No." Adam shrugged. "I mean, yeah. Kind of. I mean, it's really okay if we can't afford a lot of stuff this time around. If you want, Santa could just bundle our gifts all together into one big present or something."

Jack flashed Sheryl one of those I'm so proud of my kids smiles.

"Now, there's a good idea. I can't see how the big, jolly fella can argue with that. In fact, I've got it." Jack snapped his fingers with an idea. "How about a set of encyclopedias? Why waste time surfing the net? You'll have all the information you'll ever need, right at your fingertips."

Michelle moaned, and Adam's shoulders sagged as the waitress arrived to distribute the drinks and hand out straws.

"What's cyclopedia?" Kim struggled to wrap her tongue around the long and cumbersome word.

"It's where someone printed out all the information from the computer in alphabetical order and bound the works in a book," Adam explained.

"A lot of books," Michelle put in.

Now Jack found himself speechless. "Now, wait, it's not exactly like that …" but Michelle and Adam weren't paying attention. They were showing Kim how to make paper snakes from the straw wrappings.

"Oohhhh!" Kim squealed as a drop of water from Adam's straw caused the scrunched up paper to unfold like a slow wiggling worm.

Jack looked to Sheryl who was watching the children. "Remember when you showed Adam how to do that?" She looped her arm through his and leaned her head against his shoulder.

"But that part about the encyclopedias being printed out—" He felt her shoulder shake in a giggle and put his head close to hers. "Do you think he's playing with me?"

Sheryl squeezed his arm. "He's playing with you, Jack."

Just as the paper snakes became too drowned to provide Kim with further entertainment, the food arrived. Steaming individual pizzas were placed in front of Adam, Michelle, and Kim. Sheryl welcomed the hot plate mounded with angel hair pasta with seafood in cream sauce while Jack gazed appreciatively at the small, steaming casserole dish overflowing with cheesy, meaty lasagna.

The kids "oohed" and "aahed" over the full dishes. Jack reached for Sheryl's hand on his right and Michelle's on his left, Adam and Kim followed suit, and the Bakers held hands in a family circle and bowed their heads.

"Lord," Jack prayed, "we are thankful for this meal you have provided. We truly understand that everything we have is a gift from you. We are thankful for you, and for each other. Please continue to provide for us and protect us. Amen."

For several minutes, conversation paused while each family member gave his or her full attention to the delicious food. Using his napkin to wipe tomato sauce from his mouth, Jack took up the topic again.

"All right, you kids want to know the truth?"

Mouths full of pizza and eyes on their dad, Michelle and Adam bobbed their heads. Quick to copy her older siblings, Kim nodded, too.

"The truth is," Jack began slowly, and paused for effect. He took a moment to make eye contact with each child and then his face lit up. "This is going to be the very best Christmas ever."

Later that night, the Bakers entered their house, laughing and exhausted. Sheryl gave Jack a kiss. "I'll tuck in the kids, Mr. Marketing Executive. You go relax."

He took a moment for each child as they passed him to go up the steps. He bumped fists with Adam, hugged Michelle, and picked up Kim to receive one of her sloppy kisses. He smiled at the joy he saw on his wife's face.

"Goodnight, kids," he called up the stairs.

He wandered into the kitchen to put the leftover food into the fridge. He felt a deep sense of satisfaction. The phone rang. He looked at his watch and then at the phone. In frustration, he picked up the receiver and immediately hung up. "Oh, call it a night, it's ten thirty."

Right then, he noticed the answering machine was blinking. Perhaps he had been hasty. Maybe Sheryl's mom needed them. He pressed the button, and proceeded to skip through a series of collection calls, deleting them as quickly as they started. Soon enough, he would have these paid up to date again. For the first time in months, he felt the sweet, soaring sense of hope. Mechanically, he listened to the beginning of each message and pressed the delete button. Until one call caught his attention.

"Yes, this message is for Jack Baker. This is Rod Stevenson with Puriease Headquarters in Madison, Wisconsin. We've been trying to reach you by cell phone but it appears that your number has changed. We are interested in talking with you about a marketing position with our company. Please return this call at your earliest convenience. Thank you."

Jack's mouth dropped open as he listened to the words. He looked up. Sheryl stood in the doorway, shock registering on her face as well.

"What are you going to do?" She came and slipped her hand in his.

"I don't know."

She looked worried. "You're not considering it, are you?"

He shook his head. "Not a chance. We've lived in Wooded Falls our whole lives. The day you and I moved into this house, we agreed that this was where we'd raise our family. We're not going anywhere—but it's nice to know we're wanted, and the offer might make a good bargaining chip if Fergusson tries to short me on my Christmas bonus."

"When it rains, it pours." She rested her head on his chest.

Holding his wife, Jack was content to be in harmony with Sheryl. To spend an evening laughing with his children and celebrating the future once again.

Swaying gently in his arms, Sheryl put words to his thoughts. "Things are finally turning around, baby. We're going to be just fine."

Chapter Thirty-three

MONDAY, DECEMBER 19, 2011

At work at Arctic Artie's on Monday, Jack wore a perpetual grin. He couldn't help himself. The lunch rush was over and as he wiped the counter, he felt peaceful and satisfied for the first time in months.

The bell over the door jangled and Jack glanced up to see Wesley come in. He checked his watch. The hour was unusually late for a lunch break at Smythe-Andersson.

"Wesley. What's the word?" Jack didn't like the gloomy expression on the man's face and mentally clutched at his newfound hope.

Wesley's words dropped like cubes from Arctic Artie's ice dispenser. "Why don't you tell me?"

Jack frowned. "Tell you what? What's wrong?"

"What are you trying to do to me?" He raked a hand through his slick hair. "I stick my neck out for you and you kick me in the throat? I swear, this is why I only do nice things for myself."

"What are you talking about?"

Wesley leaned over the counter. "Word on the street is that you've been talking to Puriease. Please make the headache go away by telling me that it's not true."

Jack took a step back. Puriease had called him, after all. "What? No. I mean, they left a message on my machine, but I never called them back." He was aware that his voice was taking on a desperate edge.

"What was all of that drivel I've heard about you never leaving Wooded Falls?" Wesley's voice held a note of betrayal. "Why would you do this to me? Fergusson is furious. I can't even be there right now."

Jack frantically shook his head. "I have no intention of leaving Wooded Falls. I am completely dedicated to coming back to Smythe-Andersson."

Wesley narrowed his eyes as he searched Jack's face for any form of hesitancy. At last, he nodded. "Then end it. Make it clear to Puriease that you neither are, nor will you ever be interested in working with them. They are enemy number one and as long as Fergusson thinks you're talking to them, there's no way you're ever coming back to Smythe-Andersson."

"All right." Jack felt like a scolded puppy. "I'll tell them I'm not interested."

Wesley leaned close and spoke with certainty. "Make it final. If this bridge isn't burned, Fergusson will never take you back."

Jack placed his palms flat on the counter. "Done. Tonight. As soon as I get home."

Wesley looked grim. "I'm counting on it, Jack. Yours isn't the only job on the line anymore."

That evening, Jack stood in his kitchen listening to the Puriease message again. It's a great company but not worth risking my position at Smythe-Andersson.

Relocating to Wisconsin had never been part of the long-range plan for the Baker family. Sheryl's mother was here, their friends were close by, and they had purchased this house as the one they would grow old together in.

He picked up the phone.

"Hi, can I speak with Rod Stevenson please? Hi Rod, this is Jack Baker … Yeah, hi … Yeah, that's why I'm calling. I just wanted to thank you for thinking of me, but unfortunately, I'm going to have to pass. Yeah, I've just got a few irons in the fire right now, and I'm really not interested in moving my family out of the area. I'm sorry … Hey, I appreciate that. I really do. I wish you guys well. You're doing some great things. Thanks again for the offer. Yeah, happy holidays to you, too. Bye."

Slowly he hung up the phone. With a push of a button, he erased the recorded invitation from Smythe-Andersson's competitor and the immediate solution to the Baker family's financial and emotional slump. He hoped this was the best decision. He knew his bridges were burned when he heard the message machine mechanically report, "All messages deleted."

Chapter Thirty-four

TUESDAY, DECEMBER 20, 2011

Sheryl made her way back to the food stamp office. The idea she would only have to visit the government agency once, receive a magic supply of grocery shopping power, and never have to come back to this humiliating, airless place devoid of hope was probably a fantasy. But that was the problem, the promised food stamps had not arrived.

So Sheryl had steeled herself to repeat the trek to the storefront in the aged strip mall. Kim was awake this time, so Sheryl read Dr. Seuss rhymes for forty-five minutes until they were once more escorted to Janice's cramped and colorless cubicle.

As Janice bent over paperwork, Sheryl glanced about the small workspace, something she had been too nervous to do on her previous visit. For a moment, Sheryl wondered about the woman who worked here five days a week and spent all day seeing people just like Sheryl, one right after another. Well, maybe not just like Sheryl. This situation was only a temporary setback for the Baker family. She imagined others probably experienced longer times of need.

Sheryl guessed that at one time Janice was idealistic about making a difference in the world, about giving people a hand up. A photo of Janice with her family caught Sheryl's attention, and she chided herself for not even thinking of Janice as a human being the last time she sat in this same chair, waiting. A woman with children and a real life outside this dreary partition.

Sheryl picked up the photo for a closer look. "Are these your little ones?"

Janice looked up, her surprise quickly transitioned into a warm smile as her gaze went to the grinning faces in the frame. "That's Andrew, Thomas, and our little Megan. Well, she's not so little anymore."

Kim pulled Sheryl's arm down so she could look at the photo. Kim pointed at Megan. "Pretty," she proclaimed.

"They are beautiful," Sheryl agreed.

Janice's smile disappeared as she stacked the papers in Sheryl's file. "I imagine you're here because you haven't received your food assistance card."

"I hate to seem impatient, but the card was supposed to come around the middle of the month, and, you know, Christmas is next week ..." Sheryl heard the plea in her words.

"Unfortunately, we've run into a problem with your account. I tried to telephone several times, but no one answered the phone."

"We don't answer the phone these days." How strange that such an explanation didn't appear out of the ordinary to Janice or herself. "What kind of problem?"

Janice pointed to a line on a form. "It says here you have two cars."

"That's a problem?"

"Not per se. The issue is one is completely paid off, making the car an asset which you fully own."

"Okay?" Sheryl sat forward in her seat. "I don't understand."

"If you own over $1,000 worth of assets, your family doesn't qualify for assistance through this office."

Still holding the framed family photo, Kim climbed up on her mother's lap. Sheryl leaned around her daughter's dark ponytail to see Janice. Kim's hair smelled like this morning's shampoo. "We own the car, but it's not putting any food in our kids' stomachs."

"I understand."

"We owe forty thousand in credit card debt." Sheryl could hear the desperation in her voice. "Does that offset anything?"

"Unfortunately, we don't acknowledge debt in determining eligibility. Just assets."

Mentally running through scenarios, Sheryl grasped for some way to fit into their eligibility standards but came up empty. Nothing made sense. How could she play the game when she didn't know the rules? "What do you suggest? How can I find a way to feed my children?"

"If you want to sell the car and put the money toward your debt, we could reevaluate your case after that point," Janice said.

Sheryl stared at her. "Sell our car? How long might that take? The transaction could take weeks and the kids need to," she dropped her voice, "eat. Please, they need to eat today."

Janice was quiet, and Sheryl choked back tears of frustration before trying another line of reasoning. "If we sell our car, how would my husband get to work?"

"We would provide you with city bus vouchers."

"Just like you provided food stamps? We could sell the car and find there is still some reason why we don't qualify. Then we won't have food or transportation." She was embarrassed at the vileness she heard in her own voice. "Besides, won't giving my husband bus vouchers cost the city more tax dollars? Right now our transportation is not a burden on the city."

Janice nodded her acknowledgment of Sheryl's simple logic.

Sheryl continued, "And how would I get the children to school, church, the doctor and dentist? How would we get to the grocery store when we ever qualify for food stamps?"

Kim patted her mother's cheek, concern in her eyes, and Sheryl realized she needed to put a cap on her emotional meltdown. She took a deep breath. "Wouldn't it make more sense for us to keep our car and pay for our own transportation?"

"Only if you owe money on them."

"Which would mean at this point in our lives, they would get repossessed because we don't have money and can't make payments. If we could make car payments, we could go to the grocery store. If we could make car payments, we would have priorities upside down for us to pay for a car while our children went without meals. Would your office give us food stamps if we were using our money to pay on a car loan rather than feed my children? Can I qualify for food stamps if I owe on a new Jaguar?" She bit her lip to stop herself from ranting.

"The way it is," Sheryl continued, "we don't owe money on our car. We worked hard and steadily paid one off and planned to keep the vehicle for a long time. Our next goal was to pay off the second car and the house, get free of all debt and maintain good credit. Except presently our credit is in shambles, and we won't be able to buy a car again for a very long time. Selling a fully owned vehicle now, that is not worth much anyhow, certainly not any more than a year's worth of bus passes for my husband, would further cripple his ability to get a job."

"You'll just need to come in once a month, so that we can review your income status, and make sure you're still eligible," Janice outlined.

Sheryl was about to say she couldn't wait to make that pleasant experience a normal part of her regular routine, sitting here while the forms and policies searched for additional reasons why the Baker family would not qualify this time for that aid, when Kim pointed to the children in the photo.

"Sister," she said. Then she pointed to the boys. "Brother."

"Yes, Kim," Sheryl's voice softened. "Sister and brothers."

She looked back to Janice. "So if we get a little ambitious and make too much money, you'll take the bus vouchers away?"

Janice shrugged. "You have to remain eligible in order to continue receiving assistance."

"And if we've sold our vehicle, we're left with no way to get to work, so in essence, we have no choice but to keep our income below poverty level. You're actually deterring us from providing a better quality of life for our family. This office will mandate that we stay stuck where we are now in addition to not having our car."

"The system has its flaws, just like anything else." Janice studied Sheryl over her glasses. "I understand your point, and I'm not arguing its validity, but these are the rules."

Lifting Kim off her lap, Sheryl told the preschooler to give the photo to Janice. Then Sheryl stood, gathered her coat and purse, and took Kim's hand. "I misunderstood. I thought the system was designed to help hard working families who needed a temporary boost. But this is designed to trap people into giving up. In order for the rest of us to get any help, we have to become completely dependent on you, even though that situation costs the city and hard-working taxpayers more of their hard-earned dollars. How can you help us be financially responsible when these rules are not responsible with the taxpayers' money?"

The serene picture of the shopper exchanging her food stamp card for a cart full of groceries that would feed the Baker children for a week flashed into Sheryl's mind, and she nearly choked comparing the cruel irony of reality to what she had imagined the opportunity to be. "You're creating broken, dependent people that you control and manipulate into unproductive deadweight on society. How does that benefit our community or the individuals in the system? We complain about people living off of the system, but you're keeping them there. You know what? Keep your little stamps."

Sheryl stormed toward the door, calling back over her shoulder, "Merry Christmas."

Chapter Thirty-five

The all-business clicking of Miranda's stiletto heels immediately ceased when she stepped into the deep carpet of George Fergusson's office. In one hand, her fingers with long, lacquered nails were wrapped around a can of Beautiful Blue. Her other hand clutched a folder. She stopped beside the oversized, highly polished desk.

Concentrating on the stacks of reports, Mr. Fergusson didn't look up. She knew he knew she was there.

"Sir?" She moved a mug of cold coffee and laid the file at his elbow.

"Yes?" His eyes remained on his work.

"We've noticed something interesting about the problematic Beautiful Blue labels and—"

He scowled at her. "I told you that I don't want to hear any more talk about those bottles. That mess is behind us. Let's focus on the future." He returned to his documents, dismissing her with a flick of his hand.

Miranda held her ground. "I understand that, sir, and I'm sorry to bring the sensitive issue back up, but I've been looking at the artwork, and there appears to be a problem."

He threw down his pen. "We're all quite aware of the problem."

"There were minor changes made to the label design before they went to print." Miranda opened the folder and extracted several drawings. She arranged the artwork on Mr. Fergusson's desk and handed him a bottle with the bad label. "Nobody knows who made them."

"Is there a point to all this?" Impatiently, he picked up the ink pen and clicked it.

"These are the approved proofs." She pointed to the pertinent lines. "No typos. Yet, on the product that shipped, there are slight variations to the design."

Fergusson studied the documents. "Including the misspelling."

"Exactly."

"Strange." Forgetting the pen, Mr. Fergusson rubbed his chin. "Could someone hack into our system and alter the design? Puriease?"

"Industrial sabotage is not unknown." Her brow furrowed. "But why change the design? That doesn't make sense."

"Who else would have access?"

Miranda considered. "Maybe someone in house tampered with them."

Mr. Fergusson steepled his fingers under his chin. "I need to think about this."

Chapter Thirty-six

Arriving back home, Sheryl unbuckled Kim from her car seat and slammed the van door with more force than was necessary. She brimmed with anger at the whole situation, Jack's loss of a job and inability to find work with an adequate income, and now the government's ridiculous system. Weary of the weird meals she had pieced together from the rapidly dwindling food in the pantry and freezer, she longed for fresh vegetables. Though no one had complained, she suspected the children would even be happy to see broccoli on their dinner plates.

Entering the house, she helped Kim with her jacket and tossed her own coat onto the hall tree. A few more steps took her to the living room where she stopped in amazement. Adam and Michelle laughed at her open-mouthed astonishment. They danced around her chanting, "Surprise, surprise."

Keeping with tradition, the Bakers had dutifully put up both Christmas trees the weekend of Thanksgiving. Jack and Sheryl's hearts hadn't been in it, but they didn't want to disappoint the kids. Colorful keepsake ornaments—that each child received new each year—decorated the tree in the family room.

A tree ten feet tall occupied the vaulted living room. The smaller seasonal touches including new candles, fresh holly, and the usual row of giant poinsettias were conspicuously absent from the fireplace ledge, but the room looked reasonably festive. But that wasn't what made Sheryl catch her breath.

The room had been transformed with long strands of handcrafted paper decorations. Strings of unlit Christmas lights looped along the edge of the fireplace mantle and around the china cabinet. The children had obviously spent hours creating the decorations and digging through boxes from earlier Christmases for leftover light strands.

She sank down into a wingback chair. "Oh, my. Kids, this is amazing."

Michelle's eyes danced. "Adam hung the lights. I made the decorations. Do you like them?"

"I love them." Sheryl hugged her daughter, relishing the sound of Michelle's delightful laugh.

"Pretty." Kim held out her arms and spun in circles. "Pretty."

"This room has never looked so beautiful," Sheryl agreed.

"Wait until you see the bulbs all lit up." Adam crossed to the light switch. He dimmed the room lights and plugged in his masterpiece.

Instantly the room transformed into a winter wonderland. Sheryl squeezed her son's arm. "Adam, this looks very chill. I can't wait for your dad to see it."

The jarring ring of the phone disrupted the moment. No one moved to answer, but their happiness deflated like a balloon releasing air. Suddenly, the phone stopped mid ring and at the same time, the lights went out.

In an instant, the festive holiday atmosphere dissipated. In the dim gray of the winter day, Kim whimpered. Sheryl quickly knelt next to the child and pulled her close. "We must have blown a fuse," she reasoned. "Nobody panic. Adam, can you reach the lights?"

"I can reach them," he reported, "but they're not working."

"Not the Christmas lights, dear—the living room lights."

"Roger that. They're not turning on."

Sheryl did a mental calculation and groaned. "I think our power has been turned off."

Now Adam and Michelle moaned.

Sheryl blurted out the only thing she could think to say, "Well, merry stinking Christmas." She felt like crying.

The children giggled at her comment, and suddenly, the words seemed funny to her, too. Soon they were all laughing in the shadowy house.

"I'll light the gas fireplace and get candles." Sheryl made her way to the kitchen drawer where she located a couple fat candles and a rectangular box of wooden matches. "We'll be okay."

Chapter Thirty-seven

That night, Jack squinted in confusion as he turned onto his street. No welcoming glow came from the Baker house. Why doesn't Sheryl have the Christmas lights on?

He stopped the car in the driveway and gazed at the other gloriously lit houses around the cul-de-sac. He couldn't make sense of it. Not that the Bakers had put on their customary newsworthy decorating extravaganza this year—there would be no photo in the newspaper of the Bakers in Santa suits—but they had set up the basic outdoor Christmas lights and Colonial style electric candles in the windows. However, even these simple tributes to the season remained unlit this evening.

Movement caught his eye, and Jack glanced down the street to see the newspaper photographer's familiar sedan approach. He groaned. The photojournalist expected to take another great holiday picture at the Baker address. Jack slunk low in his seat, too embarrassed to be seen. Through the side mirror, he watched the car stop at their address. After a slow revolution around the cul-de-sac, the car halted again in front of the unlit Baker house. Jack had a sudden fear that the next day's newspaper would carry a shot of their dark and undecorated house with the headline, "Worst Christmas Display in Wooded Falls."

Driving slowly past the brightly decorated neighboring homes, the reporter lowered the automatic window just far enough for the oversized lens of the camera to brave the cold and snap a few pictures. Then, mercifully, he left.

Jack wanted to get inside before others began driving down their street to view the Baker's yearly award-winning holiday decorating extravaganza. Wooded Falls residents who included a drive past the Baker home as part of their Christmas celebration would be disappointed. He didn't think he could handle letting down more people right now. He took a deep breath and instantly regretted the action as he inhaled the residual onion and burger odor of Arctic Artie's on his clothes. On the visor, he pressed the button on his garage door opener. Nothing happened. He pushed the button again. The garage door remained closed.

He dropped his head onto the steering wheel, his mind blank. After a few moments he put the car in park and turned off the engine. He trudged up the walkway and unlocked the front door.

"Sheryl? Kids?" He stepped inside and felt his way toward the living room where he could see golden flickering shadows.

"Over here, sweetie." Sheryl's voice sounded gentle and tender. No tension here. His shoulders relaxed.

Jack found his family gathered around the fireplace. They wore extra layers of sweatshirts and sweaters but the scene looked cozy. Inviting. Holding her guitar, Sheryl softly strummed "O Little Town of Bethlehem." How long since she'd played her guitar? She used to enjoy making music by the hour.

Jack surveyed the cozy scene. "Is everybody okay?"

"We're fine, Dad." Adam shifted to make room for him next to Sheryl.

"Come on over." Michelle patted a place on the carpet. "Sing Christmas carols with us."

Jack slipped out of his overcoat and sat cross-legged next to Sheryl. He preferred this strange joy to the painful misery that could just as easily have greeted him. "Christmas carols? In the dark—and cold?"

Sheryl leaned against him. "It's not cold over here."

Hmm … this could actually be fun.

Kim settled onto his lap as Sheryl continued. "Adam and Michelle decorated the house. It's beautiful. You'll have to see their handiwork in the morning."

"Can't wait." Then he understood. "When did we lose power?"

"About an hour ago, but you know what? It's not that bad. We've been singing and telling stories."

"It's awesome." Adam mussed his dad's hair. "'Bout time you got here."

Michelle giggled. "This is fun, Daddy."

Jack grinned at Sheryl. "Fun? Did you put something in their juice boxes?"

She laughed. "This is where we are, Jack. Love it or hate it, this is our situation until we're able to make the situation better. I'm done hiding from what we're going through. I'm done being embarrassed. This is just one of the more interesting and unpredictable chapters in our story. I'm not going to let what's out of our control ruin another moment. We've been talking and unanimously decided that we're okay with a lean Christmas. It's just stuff."

"It's cool, Dad," Adam assured. "We don't need any big goo. We can just hang together. Try something new." Was this the same son who had insisted on computer software and electric cars and video games last Christmas?

Michelle nestled in under his arm. "Yeah, it's okay, Daddy."

Jack took in the wonder of the moment. With the firelight flickering on Sheryl's face, she had never looked more beautiful. He elbowed Adam. "Big goo? Who is your English teacher?"

"Well, you know, 'def' and 'rad' were losing momentum even back when we were using them." Sheryl looped her arm through his. "I'm sorry I got caught up in appearances. I became focused on maintaining some ridiculous image and forgot to show the most important man in my life how much I love and believe in him."

"Even if he's flipping Artie Burgers at Arctic Artie's?"

Her fingers laced through his. "Even more because I know he's serving burgers for us."

He squeezed her hand. "It just became undeniably clear to me again why I married you."

She strummed the guitar and as the Baker family sang the words of "Silent Night", the house didn't seem so dark.

Chapter Thirty-eight

DECEMBER 21, 2011

Wearing their warmest winter pajamas and adding extra blankets on the beds, the Bakers were warm enough through the night, but Jack woke the next morning determined to change their situation. Today.

Rejuvenated after last night's family time around the fireplace, Jack felt ready to tackle the world again on behalf of those he loved. Rising early, he dressed professionally and filled with optimism, picked up his keys.

Outside, he strode purposefully to the driveway and then froze. His keys fell from his fingers and clattered to the pavement. His car was gone. Missing. Vanished.

Recovering from his shock, Jack considered calling the police and then reconsidered. No doubt the car had not been stolen but had been repossessed. They had paid off Sheryl's car, but owed plenty on Jack's vehicle, and he knew they were months behind on payments.

Running his hands through his hair, he sat down on the porch. Though tempted to return to bed and pull the covers over his head, Jack pushed the impulse away. He sighed heavily and recalled the closeness his family had experienced last night. Singing and being together in their unlit house had ignited in him a new determination for their future. Mentally, he lassoed that inspiration. Back inside the house, Jack plucked the minivan keys from their peg and went to the garage.

Driving the familiar route to his old job, Jack's head overflowed with creativity. He parked and entered Smythe-Andersson Cleaners. His briefcase full of plans and sketches, Jack planned to see his ideas transformed into steady employment for him and profit for his company.

Coming into Mr. Fergusson's office, Jack was aware he had interrupted a meeting between Mr. Fergusson and Wesley. What an unlikely meeting of the minds. Had Wesley been promoted? Why would he be showing papers to Mr. Fergusson?

Mr. Fergusson appeared rattled as he struggled to his feet and shook hands with Jack. "Jack Baker. How have you been?"

"I'm well, sir, and ready to come back to work." Jack kept his voice upbeat and confident. "I can start immediately."

Back at his desk, Fergusson pushed Wesley's artwork under other papers as Jack pulled sketches from his briefcase and arranged them before Mr. Fergusson. "I've designed new concepts, and I'm ready to start filling the shelves with product. I'm hungry for this. I'll work from home for now if you need more time to clear my name with the media but let's stop losing time and start selling our new, environmentally responsible products."

Mr. Fergusson and Wesley stared at Jack. Perhaps he should have let them know he was coming. Maybe they hadn't seen him be this assertive in the past. Hunger can make a guy aggressive.

Mr. Fergusson cleared his throat. "Jack, I'd love to help you out, son, but we really can't start issuing you any checks until people have forgotten why they hate you." He looked at his wall calendar. "It could be months."

Jack looked at Wesley and then back to Mr. Fergusson. "Months? What about my Christmas bonus?"

"Well, now, that would be a check, wouldn't it?" Mr. Fergusson spoke with the condescending tone the old man used on Wesley that day when he'd gotten ahead of himself in Jack's office and made an embarrassing impression on Fergusson. Today, Jack sought employment while Wesley held a position at Smythe-Andersson.

Jack looked at Wesley, who shrugged. "I said no guarantees, Baker."

"Mr. Fergusson, I don't mean to be pushy, but I need that Christmas bonus. My power was shut off last night. Our only source of heat is our gas fireplace and that could go any day. I've got no cell phone, no cable, no internet. Collection agencies and law firms are calling every ten minutes."

Remembering the lack of electricity, he amended his last statement. "Well, they were calling until the phone service went out. Christmas is Sunday, and we don't have gifts for the kids. I need that money."

Wesley glanced at his watch. "Yeah, speaking of money, shouldn't you be prepping my lunch?"

"I quit my job at Arctic Artie's so I could be here today. I am completely dedicated to Smythe-Andersson."

"What about Puriease?" Mr. Fergusson sounded coy.

"I told them to find someone else," Jack assured. "I'm not willing to relocate the family."

Mr. Fergusson looked pleased. "You are dedicated, Jack, among other things."

Jack drew himself up tall. "Yes, sir."

Mr. Fergusson pushed a button on his desk. "Unfortunately, like I said, we just can't risk bringing you back right now. The changed design and the typo on the label were a mess. After firing you, the class action lawsuit was dropped, and we're developing a brand new public image. Things are going quite well for us. In fact, with the way profits have risen since your departure, I don't foresee ever needing you again. Turns out, Wesley here is a pretty sharp marketing guru. Must be all that time following you around." He looked at the paper on his desk. "I just wish you'd taught him to spell. There are four typos on this proof."

Wesley chimed in, "We have little people for spell-checking. You don't pay doctors to mop hospital floors."

Suddenly, Mr. Fergusson looked from the paper to Wesley. "Your spelling," he said slowly. "The label."

Jack followed Mr. Fergusson's train of thought. "Changed design and spelling errors on the label." He whirled to face his previous assistant. "Wesley!"

Eyes wide in innocence, Wesley looked from Mr. Fergusson to Jack. "What?"

Two security guards entered the room and flanked Jack.

"What's going on?" Jack demanded.

For a moment Mr. Fergusson looked confused as he considered Wesley and Jack. Shaking his head, he promised, "Wesley, you'll pay."

Fergusson then addressed Jack. "I'm sorry, son. The damage is irreparable. I know it wasn't you, but the world thinks it was. If we change that, we'll put the company at risk. If you hurry, maybe you can still get your burger job back."

Stunned by their callousness, Jack regarded Mr. Fergusson and Wesley.

Wesley shrugged. "I'd like to say I gave helping you my best effort, but that would be a lie, and, in this case, the truth is much more fun. But come on, would you have done anything differently if the roles were reversed?

We all look out for numero uno, Jack. It's what keeps the world spinning merrily 'round and 'round."

Mr. Fergusson nodded to a security guard, who firmly took Jack by the arm. "Let's go."

Jack allowed himself to be escorted from the room, but stopped in the doorway and turned back to Mr. Fergusson. "You never intended to hire me back. This whole time, you were leading me on."

Wesley choked back a laugh. "My goodness, he's just now getting it."

Mr. Fergusson's answer was harsh. "You're too trusting, Jack. That's always been your problem. You need to open your eyes, look around, and discover that nobody is looking out for the other guy—yourself included, and you know it. If you're not spending every waking moment thinking about how you can make life better for Wesley here, how can you justify the assumption that he, or anyone else, is thinking about doing anything for you? Wake up, Jack. We live in a cold world, full of self-serving individuals. If you want to stay at the top, you've always got to cover your back."

Jack was speechless as the guards accompanied him down the same hallway and past co-workers he had passed on his jubilant walk after his marketing presentation. The setting was familiar but his success seemed like an eternity ago. He felt empty and alone. And betrayed.

Chapter Thirty-nine

George Fergusson sighed. After his big lecture to Jack about being number one, he felt sick about what he had done.

His reverie was interrupted by Wesley's nasally voice. "Well, I'm glad that's finally over."

Mr. Fergusson closed his eyes, realizing he had another confrontation on his hands. Yet, he needed to keep the little twerp. He couldn't afford to get rid of him right now.

"You've got a lot of typos here, kid." He tapped Wesley's latest work.

"Right." Wesley appeared unconcerned. "I'm not the best speller in the world, but that's not why I'm here, is it? I blend colors and images into purchase-ready harmony."

From his desk drawer, Mr. Fergusson pulled the bottle with the faulty label. "It's been brought to my attention that some last-minute changes were made to this art before the project went to print. What can you tell me about that?"

Meanwhile, Jack took the long way home, pulled the minivan into the driveway and turned off the engine. He stared at the steering wheel, deep in thought and out of hope. How would he explain this new disappointment to Sheryl? They were down to one car and he'd left her carless all day without an explanation. But this new development had killed their dream for a return to their previous life.

He jerked at a knock on his car window. Their next-door neighbor, Phil Roberts, was staring in the window with a big, goofy grin.

"Hey, Baker!" he called through the glass. "What happened to all of the lights?"

Still feeling shaken, Jack opened his door and stuttered, "What?"

Phil pointed to the house. "Why wasn't your house lit up last night? The whole neighborhood is talking about it. You planning some big surprise show or something?"

Jack stepped out of the car. He wearily headed toward the front door, frantically searching for something to say. Phil followed close on his heels.

"I don't know how you're going to top what you put together last year, but you always find a way, don't you? We're all looking forward to the big display. Is that why you're not parking in the garage? Got the space all packed full of goodies?"

Jack unlocked the front door and faced Phil. There is no more hiding the truth because our embarrassing truth is no longer temporary. His voice sounded thick as he spoke. "Nope. I can't get the garage door open because my power's out. They shut it off yesterday for lack of payment. I'd turn it back on, but I don't have a job which means I'm broke, so you might want to make your rounds and let everyone know. Unless they put together some kind of 'save the Baker Christmas display' fund, there's not going to be anything to see this year. And I think we both know how many of us are willing to help a hurting neighbor at Christmastime, don't we? So, here …"

Jack knighted a speechless Phil with an imaginary sword. "You be the grand master of glitter this year." He entered the dark house and closed the door softly behind him.

Jack found Sheryl sitting quietly by the fireplace. She looked still, resigned. He dropped his jacket on a chair and sat down beside her.

"Hey, honey." He dreaded telling her the bad news.

"Hi."

"Where are the kids?"

"I sent them out back to go sledding."

He heard something in her voice that filled him with unease. "Are you okay?"

She exhaled and handed him an envelope stamped certified. "This came today."

Jack braced himself as he pulled the contents from the envelope.

"It's a notice of foreclosure." She sounded as weary as he felt.

"Notice of foreclosure." He repeated the phrase, trying to comprehend what she was telling him. His news wasn't the worst after all.

"If we don't pay them four thousand eight hundred dollars in the next seven days, we're going to be homeless."

Jack stared at the letter. He had no words.

She continued. "You're not going to get your bonus, are you?"

He turned to her in surprise. "How did you know?"

She shook her head. "I've felt it all day. Ever since I got this. When I opened the notice, I just knew. We're going to be homeless, Jack." Tears traced down her cheeks.

Jack pulled her close, but she seemed distant. He felt desperate and needed to do something quickly. "No, we're not going to be homeless. There's a way to fix this, we just need to figure it out. Can we call your mom?"

Sheryl looked incredulous. "And ask her for five thousand dollars on December twentieth? She doesn't have that kind of money."

"Well, we need to get a loan."

Sheryl gave an unladylike snort. "Who in their right mind is going to loan us any money?"

Jack snapped his fingers. "What about the church?"

Sheryl looked puzzled. "What about the church?"

"You know. Their ministry to people in the community. The thing the kids are always raising money for. The Children's Community Fund." He laughed aloud. "I think we qualify for that."

Her eyes brightened. "I think that's supposed to be for people who don't come to church, but it's worth a try."

Jack gave a whoop and stood up. "Anything is worth a try. I don't care what anybody thinks about us. We just need to get caught up."

Chapter Forty

December 21, 2011

Four days before Christmas, Jack motored into the parking lot of the church and parked. He admitted to himself that he felt odd being here on a day other than Sunday. Jack wasn't one to frequent the church like those people who were at the building whenever the doors were open. No, Jack believed that he belonged in church on Sunday and hadn't found much reason to drop by during the week.

Until now.

The parking lot looked different with only a few cars he recognized as belonging to staff members. Jack couldn't help glancing about for the kind-eyed older gentleman who shook his hand each week. He made a mental note to ask the man his name when he saw him next.

Jack entered the building and made his way down the hall. He stopped at the pastor's office and tapped on the open doorframe. Pastor Jim looked up from his computer screen.

"Jack," he exclaimed. "Jack Baker." The pastor stood and came to Jack, extending his hand in welcome. Jack blinked, surprised to see the pastor pad over in loafers, casual Dockers pants, and a roomy sweater pulled over a plaid shirt with the top button undone. Jack thought pastors wore suits every day. Probably mowed the grass in a suit. Jack accepted the warm handshake.

"Come in." The pastor waved him inside the homey office. "Would you like some coffee?"

"I would," Jack said and the pastor pointed him to the full Mr. Coffee and Styrofoam cups on a shelf near the window.

"Help yourself and come have a seat." The pastor returned to his chair behind his desk. "Deliver me from the tedium of end of the year fiscal figures."

"Not a man of numbers, are you?" Jack poured a cup of coffee.

"Give me people any day with all their foibles, eccentricities, and quirks. I thrive on relationships, ministry, and mentoring."

"Not numbers?"

Pastor Jim pressed his long fingers against his graying temples, and then lowered his voice conspiratorially. "Math, my good man, is a four-letter word."

"So it is," Jack raised his cup. "Can I pour you some?"

"No, no, I've had my pot for the day. Trying to cut back and all that."

Locating the sugar bowl near the coffee pot, Jack searched for a spoon but didn't find one. He turned back to the pastor who frowned at the computer screen. "Sorry to bother you," Jack said, "but do you have any spoons?"

"Of course not." Pastor Jim's eyes remained on the screen. "There are no spoons at this time of year."

Jack felt himself frown. Had he missed something? "Excuse me?"

"It's Christmas." The pastor's tone suggested that should explain everything. With a twinkle in his eye, Pastor Jim looked up and met Jack's questioning gaze. "And not a creature is stirring."

Jack groaned and dropped into a seat across the desk from the jokester. He sipped the hot coffee and noted the walls of stocked bookshelves in the simple office.

"So, Jack, what brings you to see me on a Wednesday afternoon?"

"I wish I had a noble answer for you, but I came to ask for help."

The older man folded his hands on his desk and gave Jack his full attention. "What kind of help?"

Feeling his chest tighten, he began, "Well, I lost my job a few months ago."

"I'm sorry to hear that," Pastor Jim said.

"We're doing amazingly well, all things considered," Jack went on, "but we've fallen a little behind financially."

Nodding, Pastor Jim inhaled through his teeth. "That is rough."

"This is a temporary bump. I wouldn't even bother you except I found out yesterday that unless we come up with forty-eight hundred dollars, we're going to lose our house. You know me, I'm the last person to ask for help, but I've got nowhere else to go."

Compassion showing in blue eyes surrounded by deeply etched laugh lines, Pastor Jim sighed deeply. "Jack, I am truly sorry for you and your family. I wish there were something I could do to help, but there just isn't. We don't have the resources."

Feeling desperate, Jack sought a solution. "Maybe the Children's Community Need Fund the kids are always collecting for?"

Pastor Jim nodded. "That's my dream for the Children's Community Need Fund too. The program has potential, but so far not enough principal to save anybody's home."

"Why not? We donate to the fund every year."

"Presently the project is more of a tool to teach children to give than a program that is having any sort of impact on the community. We only raised $72 this year."

"Seventy-two dollars?" Jack whispered, incredulous.

"And we've been approached by fourteen families just like you who are facing foreclosure."

Jack sat stunned, his hope dissolving like sugar in coffee. He realized Pastor Jim was still speaking.

"… $72 isn't going to save anyone's home so we gave the money to Feed the Needy. They'll add that amount to their bottom line and put the money to good use."

"But hundreds of kids raised money for that fund. How could there be less than a hundred dollars?"

Pastor Jim shrugged. "Thirty-seven cents at a time."

Chapter Forty-one

Coming in from the mailbox, Jack found Sheryl and the three children gathered around the kitchen table.

"What's this?" He stepped closer. "It looks like a snow storm in here."

"It is, Dad," Michelle announced. "Mom showed us how to cut snowflakes from coffee filters."

"Lookie," Kim waved a homemade snowflake for Jack to admire. "My 'noflake."

"It's lovely, honey." Jack gave her shoulders a little squeeze.

From the fireplace came the aroma and circus sound of popping corn. Kneeling on the hearth, Sheryl shook a pan over the flames. "Without electricity, it's not like we're using the filters in our coffee maker."

"This is a far better use," Jack agreed. "And is that popcorn I smell?"

Kim jumped down from her chair and ran to her mother's side. "Mommy is making 'corn."

Threading several snowflakes together to hang from a coat hanger, Adam nodded. "Mom found the popcorn bag in the same cupboard with the coffee filters. So hey, what's a mom to do?"

Jack helped Sheryl pour the hot, fluffy popcorn into a large bowl. "A bowl of 'noflakes," Kim announced, and crammed a handful into her mouth.

"How are you?" Sheryl asked softly.

Jack shrugged, his face close to hers. "How about if we skip out on this snow party and do some Christmas shopping?"

"Really? Now?"

"Why not?"

The two of them glanced at the children. Adam, Michelle, and Kim were busy snipping filters into snowflakes, taping them into snowstorms on the windows, and stringing their creations along with popcorn throughout the house. In between, they were eating and throwing the popped kernels at one another. Inside, their home was looking snowier by the minute.

"Adam, Michelle," Jack called. "You two hold down the fort for a while so I can take your mother Christmas shopping."

Adam halted from throwing a well-aimed popcorn bomb at Michelle to salute his father. "Aye, aye, captain."

Jack saluted back. "Party on."

Outside, Jack opened the passenger door for his wife. "Mrs. Baker."

"Thank you, Mr. Baker."

Leaving their subdivision, Jack began, "We've got less than forty dollars from my last Arctic Artie's paycheck. Where do you want to spend our millions?"

"Going out to dinner on Christmas Eve is another tradition that the children count on."

Jack nodded. "I admit I'm pretty floored by this whole experience. The kids are taking this in stride far better than I am. What beats all is how much happier they are just having more time with me. Having less money, even no electricity, no television, no computer, hasn't made them complain half as much as I thought it would."

"So if we get them a couple well-chosen items at the dollar store," Sheryl outlined slowly, "perhaps we can stretch the money to include dinner out tomorrow evening too?"

Jack puffed out his cheeks thoughtfully. "That means only a couple dollars each." He looked across to her. "I don't even know where a dollar store is, so lead on, Kemosabe."

Sheryl directed him to the strip mall. "I remember seeing a dollar store two doors down from the food stamp office." She stiffened as Jack turned into the parking lot and found a parking place.

"You okay?" Jack looked sidelong at his wife.

"I'm avoiding looking at the food stamp office," she explained. "I don't want the memories to color our shopping spree."

Jack nodded. Though they were genuinely having some happy times together, he was keenly aware both of them were often a single emotion from giving in to wallowing in freakish misery. He felt like a tightrope walker, balancing between the desperate hope that soon life would return to their familiar normal and feeling desolate that the Baker family had been seemingly rejected from the circle of society's normal.

Sheryl put his thoughts into words. "Even when we asked for help"—she dared a frown at the food stamp office—"we were told we didn't fit. Being a misfit is decidedly uncomfortable. I prefer being like everyone else."

Jack put the car in park and turned off the engine. He leaned forward and rested his forehead on the steering wheel.

Sheryl put a hand on his shoulder. "What are you thinking?"

"I feel inadequate to care for you and the children."

"None of this is your fault." Her voice was gentle. "We've been over this a thousand times."

"Only a thousand?" He sat up and gripped the steering wheel, his knuckles turning white. "I have less money for this than I usually spend on lunch at a drive through, let alone gifts for my kids."

Sheryl nodded. "That's a fair description."

"Do you know when I last spent a dollar for a Christmas gift?" He pounded the steering wheel to punctuate each word. "When I was eight ... years ... old."

They were silent for a while, watching shoppers coming and going from the dollar store. Jack noted that most customers looked to him like they could use an updated wardrobe.

"Honestly," Jack whispered, "going in there, I feel dirty."

"I know, Jack. I know. But there is also something … something …" She searched for the word. "Something happening in all this. I see a difference in the children. All my worst fears are becoming reality. No money, creditors chasing us, power shut off—yet behind the panic I fight to stave off, there is a peace. There is a contentment in the children, a faith that we are enough. They trust us and God to care for them." She turned to him. "What did you see when you came home today?"

Remembering, Jack smiled. "Scissors, coffee filters, paper scraps everywhere like confetti after a parade, popcorn, children, my lovely wife. All having fun together."

"That's the magic we are learning. The magic of what is really important. Of how simple life can be and the joy in simplicity." Sheryl leaned forward to peer through the windshield at the nativity scene atop the strip mall roof. "Perhaps that was why baby Jesus was born in a stable instead of a palace. From the beginning he has been showing us how important simple is."

Jack reached over and took her hand. She met his gaze and her reassuring smile told him he was not alone. They were doing this as a family. "It's hard doing this together," he said. "I can't imagine trying to do this alone."

Inside the dollar store, stacked boxes supplemented overstocked shelves to display a vast array of random merchandise. Knock-offs and name brands sat side by side between the seasonal, the practical, and the completely useless. Customers navigated skinny shopping carts through the aisles while children asked for treats. Overhead, Gene Autry sang "Rudolf the Red Nosed Reindeer" from a tinny speaker in the tiled ceiling.

"This is like an indoor garage sale," Jack observed.

Sheryl looked at him and smiled. "I hadn't thought of it that way."

"This," he declared, "is brilliant marketing. Someone had a great idea."

She followed him down the toy aisle. Dodging a toddler begging for a baby doll, he spied a package hung from the pegboard. "Man, oh, man, oh, man, oh, pete! Look at this, Sheryl! I haven't seen Silly Putty since I was a kid. Have you seen what this stuff can do with comic strips?"

She laughed. "I didn't know you were so crazy about the stuff."

"Adam will have a great time with this." He tossed a package into their cart. "The way I figure it, we can spend two dollars on each of the children. That's two gifts each, and we can still go out for an inexpensive dinner."

The toddler had begun to cry. "I'm sorry," her mama said wistfully. "I can't get that for you this time. There are other things we must have like diapers for your sister ..."

Jack looked at Sheryl, and she nodded. Reaching into his pocket, Jack took out one of their precious dollars and handed the money to the mother. "Please get the doll for your daughter."

She blushed, "Oh, oh, I couldn't take ..."

But Sheryl had already retrieved and placed the baby doll back into the toddler's arms. The child was smiling and hugging the doll. "Merry Christmas." Sheryl pushed Jack and their cart further down the aisle.

"Recalculating," Jack mimicked the GPS. "We can get one gift for each child and two gifts for all three of them. Family type gifts like games or something." He stopped in front of a bottle of Texas hot sauce designed to "burn the hair off an aardvark." He picked up the bottle. "Do you think the kids—"

"No." Sheryl took the bottle and put the condiment back on the shelf. "A family gift looks something more like a puzzle, Jack."

Then something caught his wife's attention. Touching his shoulder, Sheryl turned him to watch an elderly woman, not much taller than her cart, count her items. A box of cereal, dish soap, shampoo, a can of green beans, and a box of tea bags. Shaking her head, she put the box of cherry cordials back on the shelf.

He winked at Sheryl. They followed the woman to the cashier where the old lady carefully counted out her money. With a finger to his lips, Jack slipped a dollar and the box of cherry cordials to the cashier who added them to the lady's bag.

"Recalculating." Sheryl led him to the cosmetics aisle. In a beribboned basket, she found a perfume and lotion set. "Perfect for our Michelle."

Jack added the gift to their cart. For a brief moment, he remembered last year's shopping spree at the big box store and the two fully loaded carts they had purchased that day. The same day Fergusson had called his cell phone, and Jack had chosen work over family. "Our Michelle is becoming quite the lady, especially through all this."

Back in the toy aisle, the two settled on the giant bubble bottle with multiple blowing pipes for Kim. "We can have bubble blow-offs in the backyard," Jack suggested.

"Prizes to the biggest, the best, the most bubbles."

In the game aisle, Jack and Sheryl found five board games in one box. "No electricity or batteries required," Jack quipped. "Just add family members for hours of fun and a lifetime of memories."

"You should be in marketing," Sheryl replied.

"Should I?" He was suddenly serious. "I'm beginning to wonder just where I am supposed to be."

"I know." She patted his arm. "I know."

They made their purchases and exited the store. Jack dropped his wallet into his back pocket and stopped to zip his coat and put on gloves. "We're even sticking to our budget."

Sitting on the curb was a couple, their elbows on their knees. Sheryl noticed them and approached. "Are you all right?"

The young husband put a protective arm around his wife's shoulders. "Yeah. We're all right."

"Something we can do to help?" Jack plopped down next to the man. Noticing the young woman's tears, Sheryl pulled a Kleenex from her purse and pressed the tissue into the girl's hands as she sat down next to her.

The young woman dabbed her eyes and glanced back at the mall.

"Let me guess." Sheryl followed her gaze. "You visited the food stamp office, and you don't qualify."

Surprised, the woman stared at her. "How do you know?"

"Long story." Sheryl patted her arm.

"Skipping the story," Jack continued, "what exactly do you two need?"

"We wanted to have something for Christmas for our two kids," the man said.

Jack knew what that felt like. He looked at Sheryl and she nodded.

"Here." Jack handed the larger of their two bags to the despondent couple. "It's five. Five board games magically packed into one box. No electricity or batteries required. Just add family members for hours of fun and a lifetime of memories." He lowered his voice conspiratorially, "Which I share only with special customers like you who understand—our kids truly are having fun just playing with us."

Jack stood. Taking Sheryl's hand, he pulled her to her feet and they headed to the car. Over their shoulder they called, "Merry Christmas."

Chapter Forty-two

DECEMBER 22, 2011

A defeated Jack opened his mailbox. Three days until Christmas and tidings of great joy would be appreciated. There were a number of envelopes inside, and he attempted to fan a weak spark of hope. Just maybe there would be good news in one of the envelopes. Perhaps Fergusson had acquired a change of heart just in time for the holidays.

Jack shook his head and mentally chided himself. For far too long he had foolishly looked back to what had been. Clutched at past glory. Squaring his shoulders toward the future, he reached in. At best, there might be a Christmas card among the envelopes.

Thumbing through the bills, he found a letter from Arctic Artie's. He slid his finger under the envelope flap, paused, and pulled out his final paycheck. $38.16. He blew out a breath. $38.16 to feed my family. The impossibility of the need compared to the supply cut deeply.

Later that night, the family gathered in front of the gas fireplace in the living room. In sweatshirts, winter socks, and slippers, the five Bakers wrapped quilts across their laps. Sheryl strummed "Oh Little Town of Bethlehem" and Michelle sang softly, teaching the words to Kim. Adam stretched out, resting on one elbow. Jack felt the melancholy that crouched at the edge of the glow cast by the firelight.

"So," Jack began. "What do you remember about Baker family Christmases?"

"Like our favorite ghost of Christmas past?" Adam pointed to the basket of Christmas storybooks. Each evening, Kim or Michelle picked out a book for their mother to read aloud. A Christmas Carol by Charles Dickens rested in front of the collection of holiday titles.

Jack nodded. "Something like that."

"Remember the time when Michelle pulled the Christmas tree down on top of herself?" Adam sputtered with laughter.

"I didn't think that was funny." Sheryl looked from Adam to Jack. "More like the moment that scared me to death."

"Do you remember the look on her face when we pulled the tree off of her? She never moved." Jack tussled Michelle's hair. "She lay there with saucer eyes, trying to figure out what in the world had just happened."

Michelle began to giggle and Sheryl laughed with the others. Kim climbed into her mother's lap, smiling so big that her eyes became half-moons. Sharing a wholehearted belly laugh with family warmed the room. Jack grabbed his side in pain. "Ow! Cramp!"

As the merriment died down, Jack looked at the faces of his dear family. These had been deeply emotional months, seasoned with worry and discouragement, but also punctuated by rich moments like this. He was keenly aware of how much they had drawn together as a family.

Little Kim seemed to read his thoughts. "This is fun."

Sheryl smoothed back her daughter's hair. "I've been immensely enjoying our campfires these past few days."

"Me, too," agreed Michelle.

"Definitely rocks," Adam credited.

"If we were having a normal Christmas," Jack considered, "we'd never have thought of doing campfires. Maybe good things can come out of bad situations."

"The phone is not ringing anymore," Sheryl noted.

Adam brightened. "Can we kill the power every Christmas?"

Hardly believing his ears, Jack looked at Sheryl. To his surprise, Sheryl seemed intrigued by the idea. Was she taking Adam's suggestion seriously? "You are one strange group of human beings." He rolled his eyes. "Maybe the power won't have been turned back on by then."

"A new Baker family holiday tradition," Adam announced.

"And speaking of new traditions, the gifts aren't going to be normal this year. I know I promised you kids the best Christmas ever, but Santa's wallet is a little light this year, so ..." All of Jack's marketing skills could not dress up this situation, nor did he want to be anything but authentic with these four people who were living real life with him. The fragile good feelings of the evening seemed to be melting away. Jack felt defeated and miserable again.

"That doesn't matter, Dad." Adam spoke with quiet sincerity. "This is the best Christmas ever."

"What?" Jack frowned. "How can you say that?"

Adam continued like he had been thinking about this for a long time and needed to get the words out. "Seriously. You guys are usually way too busy to hang with us, rack-ramming about what parties we're going to and stuff. You've never given up the time to sit around and sing with us before. We've collectively chilled every day this week, and it's not even Christmas yet."

Jack raised his eyebrows. "Collectively chilled? Where do you come up with this stuff?"

Adam shrugged.

Jack was trying to understand what Adam was saying. "So being together is really that fly to you?"

"Yeah." Adam leaned closer to Jack and lowered his voice. "I mean, don't tell my friends or anything, but you guys are kind of cool when you're not acting like Captain Busy and Mother Stress." He leaned back and spoke in a normal voice. "And stick to the standards, Dad. Nobody says fly."

Jack looked at Sheryl. She appeared unduly amused by her son correcting her husband on his usage of slang. The irony wasn't lost on him considering most of Jack's marketing skills centered on cleverly spinning language. But that seemed like a different lifetime ago now. Not to be completely put down, Jack blurted, "My bad, dog."

When the family's burst of laughter died down, Jack said, "Well, if being together can make this the best Christmas ever, we may still have a shot because, unlike money, heat, and power, time is something that I currently have more than enough of."

Chapter Forty-three

Dressed in snowsuits, gloves, and boots, December 23 found the Baker family in the backyard with a free supply of snow available for snowball fights and sledding. They made snowmen and snowwomen and a choir of snow angels.

That evening they burst into the living room, shivering and wet from the day of play. They tore off their wet coats, changed into layers of dry clothing, hung the wet things to dry, and got cozy in front of the fireplace.

"Please, Lord, let the fireplace work." Jack leaned over to flip the switch. As wonderful, warm fire bloomed in the grate, they sighed in relief.

The next afternoon, Jack hunched over the want ads in the free community newspaper.

"How goes the hunt?" Sheryl came into his office and rested her hands on his shoulders.

Jack sighed. "Nothing here I haven't already been turned down for."

"Christmas Eve is not the time to be looking for a job anyway." Sheryl took his hand and pulled him to his feet. "May as well celebrate the day with the family."

With a grin, Jack put on his snowsuit and followed Sheryl outside. From oversized snowballs, Jack constructed giant snow chairs. Now Jack and Sheryl sat on their winter furniture, sipped sun-brewed mint tea, and watched their children sled down the hill.

"Merry Christmas Eve, Mrs. Baker." Jack reached for her mitten-clad hand.

"Merry Christmas Eve, Mr. Baker." She clinked her glass against his.

"Occasionally, when I'm not panicking or sinking into a bottomless pit of despair," Jack indicated his family all together in their backyard, "moments like this make me wonder if we were supposed to go through this."

"It's strange, but I feel the same way." Sheryl frowned. "Maybe we needed to learn something."

Kim ran to them, jabbering excitedly. "Parkle 'no." She opened her mittened fist and deposited a Kim-size snowball in her father's hand.

Jack admired her find. "Sparkle snow."

Sheryl watched Kim run back to the sledding hill. "She's so cute."

Scooping up a glove full of snow, Jack watched the crystals reflect the sun. "I haven't noticed sparkle snow since I was a kid."

"It's easy to overlook the simple things when you're busy pursuing the wind."

Jack sat in peace for a few moments. "Let's walk to church tonight for the Christmas Eve service."

"Walk?"

He surveyed the yard blanketed in snow like the picture on a Christmas card. "The night will be clear. The town is decorated."

"Maybe we'll see more sparkle snow." Sheryl tugged her hat down over her ears.

Jack pointed to her iced tea. "More ice?"

"Please." Sheryl extended her glass. "We may be short on heat but we've got plenty of snow and ice."

"Such abundance. The white stuff has piled all around us." Jack removed his glove, punched into the side of his snow chair, and pulled out a handful of snow. Squeezing tightly, he transformed the snow into ice for Sheryl's glass.

That evening, the Bakers bundled in coats and scarves and walked familiar sidewalks to downtown Wooded Falls. The glow of streetlights mingled with strings of tiny icicle lights strung along rooflines of neighboring homes.

"Ooooh!" Kim pointed to a house bright with holiday display.

"Lookie, Kim." Michelle pointed to a snowperson family lined up in a store window.

"This walking thing is a clever mechanism to save gas, Dad." Adam walked with his hands causally tucked inside his coat pockets. Jack thought he looked more like a teenager every day.

"And to see the sights," Sheryl added. "To get a good look at this year's Christmas decorations."

"Okay, kids," Jack announced, "where are we going to eat our annual Baker Christmas Eve dinner tonight?"

"Whoa, Dad." Adam held up his hands. "Have we got the coin for that?"

Jack slung an arm around his son's shoulders. "Nothing fancy, but we can't miss Christmas Eve dinner. It's tradition."

"Hey." Sheryl snapped her fingers. "We could go to Arctic Artie's."

"Clever," Jack said. "I was thinking of something more like the Chinese buffet."

Michelle and Adam whooped their approval.

"We haven't eaten there in months," Sheryl said.

"Then we are overdue." Jack started walking in the direction of the restaurant.

Adam and Michelle each took one of Kim's hands, swinging the preschooler every few steps. Outpacing their slower walking parents, the children were soon a block ahead chanting, "We're going Chinese, we're going Chinese."

A sudden loud crash made everyone stop. The children turned as Jack and Sheryl hurried toward them. They heard another burst of crashing and bashing, metal meeting metal.

"Mommy!" Kim called, reaching her arms to Sheryl.

"Kids," Jack's voice was calm but firm. "Stay there."

From the direction of the noise, followed by the smells, Jack could tell whatever was causing the commotion was in the alleyway between him and the children. The children had already passed across the entrance to the alley and were standing on the sidewalk of the next block. As Jack and Sheryl stepped off the curb to cross in front of the alley, Kim pulled free from her siblings and bolted for her parents.

"Kimmy!" Adam and Michelle dashed after their little sister. Jack and Sheryl quickened their pace and in a moment dropped to their knees as Kim flew into their arms.

Breathless, Adam and Michelle were right behind their sister, and in a heartbeat, the entire Baker family were together at the mouth of the alley.

With her cheek pressed hard against Jack's shoulder, Kim faced the alley. "What's he doing, daddy?"

"What's who doing?"

Kim tapped Jack's shoulder and pointed. Jack followed Kim's gaze. Along the wall of the dark alley was a row of garbage cans. That explained the smell. While the Bakers watched, an old man in tattered clothes removed the lid from a can, pulled out a plastic trash bag, and sifted through the contents until he found something and stuffed it in his mouth.

"Gross." Michelle wrinkled her nose.

Jack stood and helped Sheryl to her feet. "That could be me." He looked at Adam. "No one should have to live like that."

Kim watched the man. "Is he hungry, Daddy?"

"Yes," Jack replied. "He's hungry."

Kim put her palms on Jack's face so he looked at her. "Can he go to Chinese?"

Jack kissed her cheek. "What about it, kids? Does anybody mind if someone else enjoys the Baker Christmas Eve dinner this year?"

Handing Kim to Sheryl, Jack reached for his wallet and walked down the alley. When he reached the homeless man gumming a petrified pizza crust, the man nervously backed up, knocking over a trashcan, and spilling the smelly contents.

Jack held out his hands. "Easy. I'm safe."

The man grunted and righted the trashcan.

"How are you doin'?" Jack popped the lid back onto the can.

"Good," the man replied. "You?"

"Can I wish you a Merry Christmas?"

The man snorted. "If it'll make you feel better."

Jack extended his hand. "It would, actually. Merry Christmas."

The older man tentatively reached out his hand and received the handshake. "Merry Christmas."

When the men released hands, the homeless man stared at his palm where folded bills rested. He looked up, surprised. "What's this?"

"My family and I want to bless you with a hot meal tonight. You have a good Christmas." Jack started back to his family, still clustered at the street.

"Hey," called the old man.

Jack turned and waved.

"God bless you, brother. And God bless you, lady. And God bless you, kids. I hope you stay in school, and get good jobs at big companies that don't never shut down on you." Stuffing the money into a greasy pants pocket, the man disappeared out the opposite end of the alley.

Jack grinned as he reached his family. Adam slapped his dad on the back and the girls smiled as everyone grabbed each other in a family embrace.

"I love you, Jack Baker." Sheryl spoke into his ear.

"Where to now?" Michelle wanted to know.

At that moment, echoing through the city streets came the peal of the church bell.

Chapter Forty-four

As they entered the church, the greeter grinned from ear to ear and shook Jack's hand. "Well, hello, good sir. How are you and your family tonight?"

"We're good, thanks. How are you?"

"I can't complain. Not one bit. How's the job hunt going?"

Jack found himself strangely intrigued by this elderly man. "How'd you know about that?"

"Oh, I've been praying for you an awful lot." He tapped his temple. "God's opportunities often present themselves in disguise. Be sure to keep your eyes wide open so you don't miss it."

"I'll keep that in mind." Jack started toward the sanctuary but turned back. "Hey, what's your name …"

But the older gentleman was already welcoming others.

From the pulpit, Pastor Jim spoke about the encouragement, truth, and hope that came wrapped as a baby when Jesus was born in Bethlehem. The theme of the evening was hope, but Jack struggled to understand what hope meant to the hungry man in the alley and to the Baker family who were about to be homeless despite Jack's hard work for his employer. After singing traditional Christmas hymns, church was dismissed and the kids ran off to chat with friends.

Sheryl saw a woman from her Bible study group. "I want to see how she's doing. I'll take Kim. Can you get my coat?"

"No problem." As Jack walked to the coat rack, he glanced from person to person. If I look carefully, I see hurt. Maybe not financial, but everyone has troubles. We hide behind happy holiday faces. His heart ached for others as he realized he was not alone in his pain.

Someone tugged on his coat, breaking his reverie. Glancing down, he saw Michelle's friend. "Hi, Barbara Ann. Ready for Christmas?"

Barbara Ann nodded. "We're going to my grandma's house tonight. I get to see my cousins."

"That will be fun. I hope you have a wonderful time."

He reached for Sheryl's coat but Barbara Ann continued to stand in front of him shifting her weight from foot to foot.

When she had Jack's attention again, she handed him a wrinkled envelope. "I made Christmas cards and sold them so your family can have a good Christmas."

"For us?"

Barbara Ann nodded. "You can open it."

Lifting the flap, he found the envelope was packed with small bills. He quickly counted. One hundred dollars. Stunned, he looked back at Barbara Ann.

"Merry Christmas, Mr. Baker." She turned and skipped away.

Jack stared at the envelope, dumbfounded. He fought the emotion welling behind his eyes and quickly slipped out of the church. Heavy snowflakes filled the air as Jack walked toward the parking lot, wiping tears from his eyes. He stopped, suddenly remembering they had walked to church.

"Good sir, are you okay?"

Jack recognized the voice of his friendly greeter. He struggled to regain his composure. "Yeah, I'm fine. Thanks." He took a deep breath to steady the shake he heard in his voice. "How are you?"

Mr. Friendly Greeter's eyes were full of warmth and wisdom. "Are you fine, Jack? Truly?"

Jack tried, but couldn't remember formally meeting the man who stood before him. "How do you know my name?"

"I know a lot about you, son."

Jack stared across the parking lot where families called Christmas greetings to one another before getting into their cars and driving away. "Yeah? Then you know that right now my life's not impressive. I'm not really interested in talking about it, and I don't think you are, either, so why don't we go back inside, and warm up?"

"Or maybe I'm just a kindly old man who cares."

Jack scuffed his shoe in a patch of dirty snow. "We can fake interest for thirty seconds or so, but deep down, nobody really cares about what anybody else is going through. We all have our own problems."

The man moved closer. "How would your life be different if one person cared enough to make personal sacrifices on your behalf?"

Jack shook his head. "Even if people like that existed, they'd pass me by. I have no job, no money, no heat, no food, and no Christmas presents for my kids. I'm standing in a freezing parking lot, spilling my guts to a complete stranger. Even more absurd, I just became keenly aware of how selfish I am. An eight-year-old kid just gave me a larger gift than I've given to any stranger or cause in my entire life. Total. I'm a complete failure."

The stranger placed his hand on Jack's shoulder. "You're not a failure, Jack."

"Really? Because I'm also going to lose my house in a few days." He was annoyed with this well-intentioned stranger. "My family, the people I'm supposed to protect and provide for, is going to be homeless. Homeless! Show me a winner who caused his family to be homeless for Christmas."

The man grinned and nodded over Jack's shoulder.

Jack turned to see the life-size nativity scene next to the church. The baby Jesus caught his attention and a moan escaped his lips. "But he was here to change the world. I'm just trying to pay for a house I can't afford."

"You are discovering your ability to make a positive impact of your own. Tonight, in the alley, you showed your children how to give. That's a greater gift than any video game or doll."

Following the greeter's gaze, Jack saw Adam speaking with an elderly woman. She shivered in a worn jacket that wasn't nearly warm enough for the cold weather. Adam had pulled off his mittens and was insisting she take them.

Jack's swallowed back insistent tears. Here I go again. Blubbering. And this time because my boy has become a kind, generous young man despite my earlier example.

"People follow your lead, Jack," the stranger continued. "You're not here to pay a mortgage or even sell cleaning supplies. You're here to be that person who genuinely cares about others. It's time to stop wishing for circumstances to be different and start becoming."

"How did you know about the alley?" Jack turned back to the greeter but the man was gone. Jack scanned the parking lot but saw no movement. He looked down. There were no footprints in the snow.

Returning to the church, Jack pondered what had just happened and the man's words. God's opportunity knocking?

Sheryl came to his side. "Jack, honey, are you ready?"

He was glad to see she had found her coat and the children were with her. His wife, his family, were gorgeous. Their walk home would be the first step on the adventure of a lifetime. The adventure of being a positive influence in the world.

Chapter Forty-five

DECEMBER 25, 2011

Christmas morning, the Baker family gathered around the unlit tree in the living room. Natural light poured in through the room's large windows, and Sheryl thought the effect was soft and serene.

Dressed in heavy winter pajamas, they had bypassed the usual hoopla of videotaping the avalanche of kids coming down the stairs and around the corner to the fully loaded tree. The small arrangement of gifts under the tree was a stark contrast to previous years. This entire year was entirely different to anything she had experienced before in her life.

No hot chocolate or coffee this year; the family sipped orange juice. OJ stayed cold in the garage.

Jack distributed the gifts and Sheryl leaned over to Adam. "How about you get us started?"

As he always did, Adam picked up his package and shook the contents. But instead of gleefully guessing what was inside, her son looked tense.

His serious demeanor knifed Sheryl's heart. "What's wrong, Adam?"

"I was just thinking." He looked from the wrapped gift to his parents. "Would I hurt your feelings if I gave my present away?"

"I know the gifts are inexpensive and you're disappointed," Jack said in an embarrassed rush.

"No, Dad. It's not that. Really," Adam assured. "I know I'll like my gift. But there is someone I'd like to give it to."

"You want to give your gift away?" Sheryl searched her son's eyes. "To who?"

"There was a kid named Nick at church last night. He doesn't have any parents." Adam shrugged. "He lives with his grandma, and she doesn't have money for presents."

Sheryl looked to Jack and saw tears in his eyes.

Michelle reached for her gift. "I want to give mine to someone who won't get a gift, too."

Kim glanced from her brother to her sister. She picked up her gift. "Kim, too."

Everything was moving so fast. Sheryl was at a loss for words.

"I don't want you to do something you will regret." Sheryl spoke hesitantly, trying to choose appropriate words.

"The gifts aren't that bad." Jack gave her a sidelong glance. "Well, comparatively, they are that bad. But at least there are gifts for Christmas."

Adam nodded. "That's exactly the point. We have gifts."

Michelle added, "And we have family."

Jack studied Adam. "You just met this kid last night. Are you certain you want to give him your Christmas present?"

Adam gave him a "duh" look.

Sheryl wanted to be certain her children knew what they were considering. "Why?"

"So he can have a better Christmas."

Jack put his arm around Sheryl. "Adults shouldn't be teaching children how to give. They should be learning from them."

Sheryl swallowed against a lump in her throat. "Is there something you do want for Christmas?"

The children seemed to reach a decision without speaking. Michelle spoke for the trio. "Can we sing Christmas carols by the fireplace?"

"I'd love to." Sheryl reached for her guitar. "With all my heart."

Soon, they were settled around the fireplace singing their litany of favorite carols when with a whispering poof, the fire went out. The gas was gone. They all stared where the cheery flame had danced moments ago. Sheryl sighed at this next adjustment for their family. How would they meet this new challenge? This additional disappointment? On Christmas day, no less.

"Well," Jack said dryly. "I finally know what to do with that box of fake logs in the garage."

After a burst of laughter, Sheryl strummed a chord and they returned to their singing.

Chapter Forty-six

Jack crossed off the date on the calendar. December 28. He took down the calendar from the refrigerator and put it in a box.

"Just toss it." Sheryl indicated the "not to be packed" pile. "It's not worth keeping."

With a flip of the wrist, Jack deposited the calendar in the trash. "Anything else?"

Sheryl shook her head. "I made a final pass through all the rooms, and we packed everything that goes." She nodded toward the remaining box the calendar had almost gone into. "That's the last one."

"You grab that, and I'll haul out this trash bag."

"Deal." She balanced the box on one hip and shouldered her purse on the opposite side.

Following Sheryl outside, Jack closed and locked the front door of their dream home. During these lean months, they had liquidated their savings and investments and sold household items to fund the basics of food and gas. In recent weeks, to pay for the rental of the moving truck, they downsized their remaining belongings to what was carefully stacked inside the smallish truck backed into the driveway.

After depositing the bag in the trash can, Jack loaded the final box in the truck. He closed and secured the rear door and pulled Sheryl close. Adam and Michelle were pelting each other with snowballs while Kim put the final touches on a snowman in the front yard. They watched the children for a few moments, and Jack recalled the years of memories they had made at this address. When Jack heard a sniff, he glanced down to see tears on his wife's cheeks.

He tightened his arms around her and pressed her face into his shoulder. "We had good years here."

He held her as she sobbed against him. How many times in their marriage had he not known what else to do except hold her? And each time he had done just that, holding her had been exactly the right thing to do. "I'm sorry," he whispered against her hair. "This was not how I planned things to go."

He felt the movement of her shoulders shift from weeping to—was she laughing? He bent to meet her eyes.

Sheryl wiped at her tears that fell while she laughed. "You know, some days I thought we would be in this home forever, and other days, I was afraid we would be in this house forever."

He cupped her face in his palms. "I love you, Sheryl Baker." He kissed the tears on her cheeks and then kissed her full lips. It was a long, tender kiss, each of them finding security in the other.

Until a snowball smacked them back into the present. Jack inhaled at the sudden cold against his cheek, and he and Sheryl turned to see Michelle, eyes wide with her mittened hands over her mouth.

"Nice aim, Michelle." Adam taunted with a cocky grin. "Even playing against me, you're the best player on my team."

Jack smiled and brushed snow from Sheryl's hair. "All right, all you softball players, gypsies, and nomads. Load up and let's hit the road to your grandma's house."

"Gypsies and nomads." As the children got into their seats and seatbelts, Sheryl took a last long look at their home. "I feel like Sarah when Abraham said they were leaving their home for a land they 'knew not of.' The unknowing, the uncertainty of what's next is unsettling."

Jack looped his arm around her shoulders. "You feel insecure?"

"Don't you?"

"Probably like Columbus whose ships were running out of food, his crew was ready to mutiny, and he was almost certain they would not fall off the end of the world. Almost."

Sheryl kissed his cheek. "Time to set sail."

"To ports unknown." Jack climbed into the cab of the rental truck where Adam was already in the passenger seat. Behind them, Sheryl drove the minivan with Michelle and Kim. The two vehicles navigated out of the driveway, away from their long-time address and history as the Crown of the Cul-de-Sac, and down the road to their next adventure.

Chapter Forty-seven

On a Saturday morning, several weeks later, the Bakers crowded into Grandma's kitchen to prepare breakfast. Sheryl poured juice and coffee while Michelle and Kim set the table. With an apron tied around his waist, Adam manned the grill next to his dad, the two men frying bacon and eggs. Grandma was at the stove flipping country flapjacks from an iron skillet onto a platter.

"You may not live in the country anymore, Grandma," Adam said, "but you still cook like you do."

"You can take a girl out of the country, but you can't take the country out of the girl." Grandma poured pancake batter from a crock pitcher into the skillet.

Still holding the coffee pot, Sheryl leaned against the antique hutch and looked out the back window at the townhouses clustered around the man-made lake. After Grandpa died, Grandma had sold the farm and moved into town. Still surrounded by many of her favorite heirloom furnishings, she had traded the work-intensive farmhouse for this new two-bedroom condominium in the middle of a modern community.

The decision to move had been a tough one. For several years, Grandma had remained on the family land while a neighbor farmed her acreage. Sheryl missed the fields of winter wheat like a thin green carpet showing through the patchy snow that wouldn't melt until the temperatures rose. She remembered the creek that bordered one side of the farm and watered the cattle pasture ringed by an old fence that attracted artists and photographers.

There had been an auction to sell everything in the big red barn that housed the green tractors and a large combine the neighbors shared each year at harvest time. When they were younger, Adam and Michelle had played on the swing that hung from the high barn rafters and jumped in the mountains of sweet golden hay. The large Percheron horses that had contentedly eaten their oats in stalls every night were now just a warm memory.

Sheryl felt a hand slip into hers and looked down to see Kim looking up at her. The barn cat that, like Grandma, had transitioned to the city and now shadowed Kim, rubbed against Sheryl's leg. Sheryl set the coffee pot on the table and lifted her daughter so the little girl could see out the window. A handful of Canadian geese flew overhead, the ones in the rear of the vee calling encouragement to the leader who did the hard work of cutting through the wind for the others.

"I wonder where they are going," Sheryl said into Kim's hair. "I wonder where we will go."

There was a knock at the front door. "Now, who could that be?" Grandma wiped her hands on her apron and went to the living room to answer the door. After several minutes, the conversation in the other room grew louder and voices could be heard in the kitchen.

"Penny, the housing association rules state that guests can only stay for the specified time."

"My family is my business, and my home is my business." That was Grandma. "And it's Mrs. Poore to you."

"Now, Penny—" The visitor's voice sounded suddenly patronizing.

"Mrs. Poore." Grandma reminded levelly.

There was a pause. Sheryl imagined her mother with her arms crossed, daring others to meddle in her affairs.

"Be that as it may, Mrs. Poore, rules are rules."

"Mama," Michelle came to Sheryl's side. "Do we have to leave again?"

"Sounds like we're getting the boot." Adam whistled softly. "You gotta admire anyone who takes on Grandma."

Still holding a spatula in one hand, Jack came and put an arm around Sheryl. He winked at Adam. "That's Grandma to us and Mrs. Penny Poore to them." He bent and kissed Michelle's worried forehead and planted a second kiss on Kim's round cheek. "No worries. We're together and everything will all work out."

Adam hooked a thumb in the direction of the front door. "And we've got Grandma Penny Poore on our side."

"Right. And that spunk runs in the family." Jack dropped his voice conspiratorially. "Do you kids know that your mom once dumped a pitcher of ice water on me? When I was in bed?"

Her three children turned eyes wide with surprise to Sheryl. "And I'd do it again." She put a hand on her hip. "In a nanosecond."

"And rightfully so." Jack tightened his embrace. "I had it coming."

From the living room came the sharp sound of the front door closing. With determined steps, Grandma returned to the kitchen and took up her station making pancakes.

"Busy bodies," she complained. "In the country, people know how to mind their own business. When folks live too close together they think proximity gives them the right to watch their neighbors and tell others what to do."

"We are grateful to be here," Jack said. "I realize it is inconvenient for you, and apparently, we've overstayed the rules."

"Pshaw." Grandma waved him away. "All in good time, Jack. Things have their way of coming together at the right time for the best reasons." She flipped a golden pancake onto a full platter. "Come and get it." Grandma set the platter on the table. "Kim, the syrup is in the pantry."

Tickling Kim so she giggled, Sheryl set her down. Purring, the calico cat followed the preschooler to the tall cupboard Grandma insisted on calling a pantry. Kim's head disappeared inside briefly and then emerged. Smiling victoriously, she carried the nearly full syrup bottle with two hands.

Grandma came and stood by Sheryl. "Everything has a season, my dear."

"Do you miss all the animals? The farming?" Sheryl sighed. "Do you miss Grandpa?"

Grandma took off her apron. "Heavens, girl! Some days I miss the farming and gardening and extry animals, but truth is, I couldn't begin to do all that again. Not at my age. Nor do I have the strength I used to. I'm better having evenings enjoying my rocking chair with biscuits and jam than bending over a garden and hot stove making the jam."

They watched Jack dish eggs and bacon onto each plate.

"Now, Grandpa is another matter. Him, I miss. We could be old together. Yet, I'm thankful for the years we had together, and I'm thankful for this time I have with you and the grandbabies. Life is all so seasonal, just like farming."

Following Sheryl's gaze outside, Grandma continued. "My one regret about selling the farm is that this cracker box condominium is barely big enough for me to sneeze without getting cat hair in my mouth. If I still had the farm, we'd have room for all of you without anyone feeling squeezed." She cast a frown toward the front door. "Nor would anyone else have a say in how long we visited."

"Mom, be honest, how are you surviving this Baker invasion?"

"Where there is room in the heart, there is room in the house. Even in a small house." Grandma clapped her hands. "Y'all sit before our vittles gets cold."

Chapter Forty-eight

Jack lifted Kim into her booster seat as everyone took a seat around Grandma's farm table that she had somehow shoehorned into the small kitchen. While a few pieces of her furniture were oversized for this downsized address, they were too much of Grandma and her history to be anywhere than with her. Wherever that was. In the same way, Jack and Sheryl had pared down their belongings to only the essentials and a few items that were important to their family. Presently, those things were stacked in Grandma's garage.

Reaching around the large table as they had so many times before, the family held hands. "Jack, dear," Grandma invited, "will you say grace?"

Clearing his throat, Jack closed his eyes. After weeks without power, he was grateful for the smells of bacon and flapjacks cooked in a heated kitchen, and the feel of the hands of his wife and daughter in his. "Heavenly Father," he began, "we are thankful for family, home, warmth, belonging, delicious food that fills our bellies, and the gift of your constant love. Thank You. Amen."

"Amen," Sheryl echoed.

As dishes were passed and people dug into their breakfast, Adam forked a helping of eggs into his mouth and closed his eyes in ecstasy. "Who'd have thought that what came out of a chicken's rear end would be suitable for sustenance."

"Who indeed," Grandma said. "For a city boy, you eat like a country kid."

Jack and Adam had served up a third round of pancakes in a contest to see who could out eat the other in Grandma's famous cooking when the phone rang. Grandma got up to answer.

Sheryl made a face. "I forgot how much I hate that sound."

Jack patted her hand. "No worries, it's not our phone."

"What if they tracked us here?" There was a hint of fear in her question.

"Relax," Jack comforted, "that's impossible—"

"Yes," came Grandma's voice behind them. "Jack is here. I'll let you speak with him."

She laid down the phone and came back to her seat while Jack sat slack-jawed, staring unbelievingly at Sheryl. "Jack, dear," Grandma said matter-of-factly, "the phone is for you."

Sheryl's eyes widened. "They did find us."

Jack stood slowly and put the phone to his ear.

Adam hummed taps until his dad rolled his eyes.

"Hello, this is Jack." He dreaded which bill collector would be on the other end. But the trepidation was quickly replaced with bright surprise. "Yes, Rod, hi! How are you? … Well, yes, I am surprised to hear from you … Yeah, we are more open to relocating these days … Sure, I could be there, well, I could be there on Monday. Thank you! … I look forward to meeting you, too. See you then."

Jack hung up the phone and turned back to the table to see all eyes on him. He waved nonchalantly at the phone. "Uh, that was Rod."

"That explains everything," Adam remarked.

Dropping back into his chair, Jack met Sheryl's intense gaze.

"Well?"

He ran a hand through his hair. "Puriease. Rod from Puriease. He said they know the problem wasn't me—about the label, I mean. They understand we don't want to move." He looked at Grandma, his gracious mother-in-law. "But they really want us to give them a shot."

Sheryl gave an excited bounce in her seat. "What are you going to do?"

"Sounds like he's going to see them on Monday," Michelle put in.

Jack nodded at his daughter. "I told them I'd be there for an interview Monday. I figure I should at least hear them out." Suddenly, lost in thought, Jack looked quizzically at Sheryl.

She met his gaze. "What?"

"They said they would double my Christmas bonus."

Grandma poured more coffee as the conversation continued.

"We will certainly spend that moolah different from now on," Adam stated.

"No doubt," Michelle agreed.

"You got that right." Jack surveyed the faces around the table. "If this works out, taking the job would mean a move to Wisconsin."

Everyone looked at Grandma.

"There is a season for everything," she said. "A season to be here, and perhaps a season to be in Wisconsin. Which, by the way, is not that far." She forked another flapjack onto her plate. "At my age, I've learned to keep my eyes open and give things a fair shot."

"Now I have to out eat Dad and Grandma." Adam groused, reaching for the pancake platter. "Kim, pass the syrup bottle."

"It will be good to get back to normal," Sheryl said.

Jack shook his head. "Let's never go back to that normal again."

Epilogue

"Jack, wait up."

Jack turned and saw Rod hurrying to catch up with him. He paused in the Puriease office's hallway to wait.

"I'm glad I caught you before you ran off to lunch." Rod handed Jack an envelope. "The board approved your request for money from our philanthropic fund for the Children's Community Need Fund."

"Thanks, Rod, this is good news."

The two began walking. "I want to know how you are feeling about your relocation here to Madison."

"Truth is, we never would have moved here if we hadn't lost our house," Jack admitted. "But now the Baker family can't imagine living anyplace else. This is home to us."

"And Puriease?"

They reached the building's large entryway. Jack stopped and indicated the life-sized nativity scene that served as the room's serene centerpiece. "I'm delighted to be part of a company that shoots straight, treats people respectfully, and contributes to the community. I like it here, Rod."

"Splendid." His boss beamed. "We had hoped to add you to the team for a long time."

The two shrugged into their coats and exited through a side door. Rod studied the winter sky. "What are your Christmas plans?"

"About now," Jack checked at his watch. "Sheryl is picking up her mom from the airport. We'll be enjoying some new Baker family Christmas traditions."

Outside, Jack heard the distinct ding-ding of a bell. "Excuse me, Rod." He turned to find the source of the familiar sound. Looking picturesque in the snow, a Feed the Needy Santa stood proudly ringing his bell outside the main entrance. Jack made his way to the front of the Puriease building.

"Merry Christmas." Jack saluted the rosy-cheeked man. "How are you doing?"

"I can't complain," Santa returned. "Not one bit."

From his wallet, Jack retrieved a generous stack of bills and pushed them into Santa's bright red pail. "This may seem like a thankless job at times," he said, "but you're doing something wonderful here. Keep up the great work."

"Thank you, good sir," Santa said. "I shall do that."

Jack started toward his car but after a few steps, slowly turned back. "Do I know you?" He shook his head. "No, it's not possible, but you look like someone I knew."

Santa leaned forward. "Did he slide down your chimney and leave gifts under the tree?"

"Good one." Jack waved. "Have a Merry Christmas."

"And the same to you, good sir."

Leaving the parking lot, Jack drove to church to drop off the check for the Children's Community Need Fund. Behind him, the front door of the Puriease building opened. Wesley, accompanied by his girlfriend, burst outside.

"I thought you said you knew people in high places here," the girl accused. "Not one person knew you. This was a complete waste of a trip to the middle of nowhere. You better get a job soon, because if I don't have enough money to get my manicure next week, I'm going to make life very miserable for you."

"More than usual?"

"What did you say? Please give me just one reason to leave you. Just one. That's all I need."

Wesley moaned as he passed Santa. His girlfriend elbowed him and stopped next to the kindly bell-ringer.

"What?" Wesley eyed the Santa distastefully.

The girl planted a well-manicured hand on her hip. "You're just going to walk by and not give him anything? Is this who I'm marrying?"

"Good grief." Wesley pulled coins from his pocket. "Here you go, Santa. Go buy some booze and cigarettes and have yourself a merry little Christmas."

Noticing a quarter in his small handful of change, Wesley dropped the coin back into his pocket. "Oops, a quarter. We don't want you getting all plastered. Creeps the kids out."

With exaggerated ceremony, Wesley dropped two dimes, two nickels, and seven pennies into the donation pail.

Santa smiled. "Thank you kindly. May your heart be forever changed from this day forward, good sir."

At that moment, a strong gust of wind blew Wesley's toupee. The hairpiece lifted and swirled above the snow in the parking lot. In mortified shock, his girlfriend exclaimed, "Well, that's new."

Wesley caught and resettled his hair before stomping back. He sneered at Santa. "I always liked the Easter bunny better."

The two young people stormed away. Santa watched them go, a merry twinkle in his eye.

Behind the Scenes

This novella, *Homeless for the Holidays*, is the novelization of a film with the same name, based on the real life experiences of writer and producer George Johnson.

"Okay, almost all of it," George admitted.

After being laid off from his job with a green cleaning company, George banked on two of his film projects moving from development into a lucrative stage. The promise of money to come was out there just beyond reach and George eventually realized he could wait for years before something happened. Before he received any income.

As unemployment stretched on, George picked up odd jobs. "I was babysitting and cleaning a guy's garage, making twenty dollars a day to feed my family of three kids. Just like Barbara Ann in the story, a young girl gave her egg money to help us out."

Before long George sunk into an emotional funk. "Most of the dialog is real. I tended to go negative, but my wife, Karen, stayed above the line. She never poured ice water on me, but she had to snap me out of it. She ripped the sheets off the bed and chewed me out. She played the guitar."

Then came the turning point. "One day I woke up," he said. "I told myself I could either sulk or do something that gives people hope."

With over forty scripts already written, George wrote another. "Most scripts take ten months to write," he explained. "Homeless for the Holidays took three weeks."

Having already produced the award-winning film, Dreamer, George set out to produce this new project. "I wasted a month looking for financing before I decided to do this on my own. But I needed a camera. Three days later, Tyler Black called. He had a RED ONE camera, better than the camera George Lukas used for Star Wars. Ty agreed to do this film on spec—that means do the work ahead and get paid after the film releases and earns money."

The usual budget for a film like *Homeless for the Holidays* is around one and a half million dollars. George kept costs to thirty thousand dollars. "In faith I stepped out with nothing but Ty and his crew on spec. We advertised open auditions in the Auburn, Indiana newspaper expecting fifty people might show. Eight hundred showed up. All together, we have five hundred people in the cast."

Including George. The writer/producer does his own acting spot in the bathroom of Arctic Artie's when Jack first puts on his penguin mascot costume. George is the arrogant customer in the men's restroom who stuffs a wet paper towel into Jack's costume.

As a salute to the Auburn movie theater where the long auditions were held, George arranged a premiere showing of *Homeless for the Holidays.* Many local residents are featured in the film including media personalities who acted as themselves in the scene where Jack opens his front door to find his cul-de-sac filled with television and radio crews. Also in the media crowd is Marsha Wright, George's friend who loaned her house—completely decorated for Christmas—to serve as the setting for the Baker family home.

Homeless for the Holidays received support from a multitude of volunteers. "There was huge amounts of volunteerism," George said. "No one was paid."

People brought food for the hard-working cast, showed up to arrange sets, and helped put things back together again after each day's filming, and at the end of the project. Jaala Wright, Marsha's daughter, was instrumental in organizing and staging scenes that were filmed in her family home.

The story resonated with the whole nation that was reeling from an economic pinch as well as with people on the set. George's wife, Karen, was a vibrant organizer during the production, bravely transparent as part of her family's experience was recorded for the world to view. Marsha Wright and her husband, Stephen, recalled an earlier time in their marriage when they had wondered how to make ends meet. Homeless, jobless, and carless, Crystal Dewitt-Hinkle who played Sheryl was living with her parents at the time of the filming.

Michael Wilhelm, the actor who played Mr. Fergusson, lived in Hollywood for two decades trying to break in as an actor. He came home to Indiana where he landed a major role in *Homeless for the Holidays.*

Matt Moore—aka Jack—was an actor in the major feature film Pearl Harbor, but wound up on the cutting room floor. Then God directed Matt to take a pastorate in the Midwest, promising, "I can make your dreams come true even in Decatur, Indiana." His career goal is that people will say to actor Adam Sandler, "You know, you look a lot like Matt."

"The kids we got were awesome," George credited. "Adam (Cole Brandenberger) was wise beyond his years. From Chicago, nearly four hours away, Michelle, played by Gabrielle Phillips, was on the set at 8:00 a.m."

Indiana native and professional comedian, Brad Stine played the crazy supermarket manager.

George Johnson has come a long way from the five-year-old who bought an eight-millimeter camera at a neighbor's garage sale and ran around making movies of everything. "The situation was a gift from the Lord. People can relate to the story because I went through this. It is experiential. It doesn't take the economy for people to limit themselves," he said. "If God is calling you to do something, he'll empower you to do it. Just start."

About the Authors

P.S. Wells

P.S. Wells is the *USA Today* and *Wall Street Journal* bestselling author of twenty-eight titles and an audio finalist. Her titles include *Rediscovering Your Happily Ever After, Bonding With Your Child Through Boundaries, The Slave Across the Street, Slavery in the Land of the Free*, and *Chasing Sunrise.*

Program producer, connector, optimistic dream driver, and sought-after inspirational and motivational speaker, she enjoys dark chocolate, Savannah Grey tea, and writing from her home in the 100-Acre Wood in Northern Indiana. Okay, it's actually five heavily-treed acres but looks like a hundred from her office windows.

P.S. is the mother of seven and "Mimi" to her grands, otherwise known as her "Grammy Awards."

Marsha Ringenberg Wright

Marsha J. Wright is the daughter of pioneer aviatrix, Margaret Ray Ringenberg, and served as her mother's speech writer, correspondence secretary, and the author of Maggie Ray, World War II Air Force Pilot. Her writing credits include short stories, articles, thirty musicals, and her mother's biography.

Wright attained her private pilot's license at age seventeen and raced with, and against, her mother in numerous air races. Her informative and inspiring presentation, Life Lessons Learned from a WASP, shares the military and racing adventures of her mother through pictures and stories with a glimpse at how the two women, different in temperament and ability, learned to work in harmony.

Wright holds degrees from Fort Wayne Bible College and Ball State University, and has studied at Jerusalem University College and Taylor University in Fort Wayne. Prior to retirement, Wright served as worship and music leader at Grabill Missionary Church, and continues to direct the area senior adult choir, Senior Saints.

She and her husband, Stephen, have five children and a pile of grandchildren. They live in Fort Wayne, Indiana.

CPSIA information can be obtained
at www.ICGtesting.com
Printed in the USA
BVHW042156261219
567936BV00014B/454/P